Heat Rises

Heat Rises

A CABIN FEVER NOVELLA

ALICE GAINES

An Imprint of HarperCollins*Publishers*

Excerpt from *Storm Bound* copyright © 2012 by Alice Brilmayer.

EPub Edition JUNE 2012 ISBN: 9780062210500

Print Edition ISBN: 9780062210517

10 9 8 7 6 5 4 3 2 1

*For Theresa. Here's to chocolate
and a glass of great zin.*

Heat Rises

Chapter One

So MUCH FOR making it to her job interview. Laura Barber might as well have been looking at a moonscape rather than a deserted mountain highway. Still shivering, she gazed out the window of the country store as the falling snow covered the pavement and filled in the road completely. The storm had started only half an hour ago. What would this place look like by morning?

"You're a mighty lucky young lady," said the shopkeeper, handing her a Styrofoam cup with steam coming out the top. "If you'd gone off the road any farther from here, you'd still be out in that."

She took a sip of the coffee and did her best not to grimace at the bitter taste. The man may be right about her luck, but she'd probably ruined her shoes on the trek here. The low-heeled pumps had cost a bundle, and she'd worn them just enough that her feet felt comfortable when she dressed for business.

"Yep," the man said as he gazed out at the accumulating snow. "Nobody'll be moving around in these parts for days."

"Mister—"

"Beaumont," he said, offering his gnarled hand.

"Mr. Beaumont," she said, studying him as they shook hands. The twinkle in his blue eyes suggested more youth than the fringe of white hair did. If you called central casting for a country store owner, they'd probably send someone like this man.

"You'd be in a heap of trouble if you'd broken down farther away," he said.

"Can someone come out and put me back on the road before things get worse?" she asked.

"You don't understand storms in these mountains, Miss."

"Ms.," she said. "Ms. Laura Barber."

"Well, Ms. Barber, won't nobody get out of here until the plows come through."

"When will that be?"

"Days," he answered. "Probably not a week, though."

"A week?" Darn it all. She was supposed to be at the bottom of this mountain by evening and at an interview in the morning. She'd planned carefully to get ahead of this storm, but her plane had landed late. Still, she ought to have been able to make her destination. She'd grown up in Connecticut and had driven in winter weather before. Snow was snow, wasn't it? Apparently not.

"What am I going to do?" she asked. "I can't stay here for days."

"That you can't. I'll be closing up and heading home in a few minutes."

"Is there a motel nearby?" she asked.

"Nope. We'll have to find a family to put you up."

"I can't impose on strangers for days."

He shrugged. "Don't see that you have much choice."

Wonderful. Not only would she not make it to her interview but she'd also have to spend days with people she didn't know. She managed well enough in business situations where procedures and rules of engagement were clearly laid out. In someone's home, she'd have to interact. She probably couldn't disappear behind her laptop without appearing rude.

"Unless . . ." Mr. Beaumont said. "Your solution might be pulling up right now."

Headlights shone in from outside—bright enough to blind her for a moment—a huge SUV or pickup, with its engine at a low roar. The motor shut off, and the lights went dim. A man climbed out and headed into the store. A blast of cold air whooshed in through the front as he entered. "Hey, Phil."

Mr. Beaumont shuffled off. "Hey, you young pup. What are you doing out in weather like this?"

"Business down in the city. Thought I could outrun the storm."

The voice tugged at her memory. Low and dark. She knew it. Even though she hadn't heard it recently enough to place it in her brain, something about the tone registered in her body.

She glanced over at the counter where he stood, his

back was to her. Tall and broad-shouldered, he commanded the space around him. She had a physical memory of that too, enough to warm her skin. Whoever this was, she'd do best to avoid him. But how?

"Good thing you're here," Mr. Beaumont said, gesturing toward her. "This lady is going to need a ride somewhere."

The man turned, and all the memory nudges turned into one huge sucker punch. Ethan Gould.

Good Lord, not him. It had to be five years . . . no, six. That night at the party. After three years of fantasies about the handsome guy who always sat at the front of the class, she'd decided to at least try to find out if the attraction was mutual. Tequila fortification, too much, had led to a night of humiliation. Oh God, all the things she'd said to him. A queasy feeling settled into her stomach remembering them after all this time.

Other than that, they'd almost never spoken to each other all through business school. He'd have forgotten her by now. Women probably came onto him all the time—women more remarkable than her. He wouldn't remember. Please God, don't let him remember.

Sure enough, he smiled at her as he would at any stranger. A genial expression he used so easily. The famed Gould charm would come next. So potent, it even worked on men. On women . . . well, forget trying to resist it.

After a moment, his brows knitted together. "Do we know each other?"

"No . . . I don't think . . . haven't met," she said. Damn it all, how could he force this reaction from her after so much time? She'd actually lie about her identity if she could get away with it. She'd avoided him successfully since that horrible night. She'd actually followed his career so that she'd know where he was. He couldn't have just happened on her on a snowy mountain, and yet, here he stood, as tempting and as terrifying as he'd been at that party.

"This is Ms. Laura Barber," Mr. Beaumont said. "You two know each other?"

"Right." Recognition dawned in his amber eyes, followed by a slight tension to his jaw. Remembering, no doubt. Her skin went from warm to burning. By now, her face would be a bright pink.

He recovered quickly, with a big smile. He still had perfect teeth, of course, and perfect skin. Only his too-large-ish ears kept him from total perfection, but the flaw made him all the more attractive.

"It's been a while," he said. "Good to see you again."

"Hi." A stupid reply but innocent enough.

"Seeing as you two know each other, won't you mind taking Ms. Barber to where she wants to go?" Mr. Beaumont asked.

He rested a hand on a nearby rack of magazines and struck a casual pose. A light of cunning in his eyes belied his apparent ease. "Where are you headed?"

"The city," she said. "I'm already late."

"How'd you get this far?"

"Rental car"—she gestured toward the outside as if she could point at the thing—"I ran off the road."

"Can't say I'm surprised," he said, his gaze never left

her face. She did her best to look straight back at him, but she'd never win a staring contest with this man. Eventually, she gave up and studied his shoes, instead. Boots, rather—the sort ranchers wore. His had a broken-in appearance, as did the faded jeans that covered his legs up to the hem of his shearling jacket.

"We won't be getting to the city tonight," he said. "But we can make it to my friend's cabin."

"Cabin?" she repeated. "In the middle of a blizzard?"

"My friend's an engineer. The place is self-sufficient with a generator and solar panels."

"The sun's not out now," she said. In fact, with the heavy snow, it was already dark.

"And storage batteries," he said. "We'll be fine."

"I haven't agreed to go with you."

"What choice do you have?" he asked, as he straightened and pulled a slip of paper from his jacket. "I'll need a few things, Phil."

"Coming right up." Mr. Beaumont took the list from him and retreated to the back of the store.

"Look, this is really nice of you—"

Before she could get the "but" out, he took a step toward her. " 'Nice' isn't exactly the word I was thinking of."

She made herself stand her ground, even though everything in her wanted to back away. "I don't want to impose."

"Don't be silly. No one around here would put someone out on a night like this."

"Mr. Beaumont said he'd find a family here to take me in."

He crossed his arms over his chest. "So, you're a social butterfly now? Happy to move in with strangers for several days?"

Damn him, he knew she wasn't. He had to remember from graduate school that she kept to herself, quietly getting top grades from her place in the back of the class.

"I . . . I . . ." Damn it. He actually had her stuttering. She took a breath. "I can't go with you."

"Why not?" he asked, as he studied her, his gaze assessing and not without a light of admiration. Her heartbeat responded, speeding up. The feeling might be pleasant with another man—one who hadn't heard about her sexual fantasies after she'd had too many margaritas. She'd told him about how her mind had wandered during boring lectures, imagining how his hands would feel on her breasts. About how she played images of him in her mind when she used her vibrator. She'd even asked if his sex was as big as she'd imagined it, and then giggled when she'd fumbled against his pants and discovered it was even larger. Oh God, humiliation. Utter and total humiliation.

"Maybe you're afraid to be alone with me," he said. He might have read her mind.

"Ridiculous." Okay, that was a lie, but she wouldn't cower before him. She'd gone on from that night to establish a good career. As a grown woman with more experience since graduate school, she shouldn't have to fear men any longer, even this one. Even if she did, she wouldn't let him know he frightened her.

"Laura, you have a choice of crowding in with a family you don't know or sharing a cabin with me. I won't even speak to you if you don't want."

"I don't think that will be necessary." Great. She'd agreed to go with him. No matter. A few days together, and she'd get away again.

"Good." He smiled yet again, the blasted man. "The cabin it is."

YOU COULD HAVE knocked Ethan Gould over with a feather. First, to run into Laura Barber at Phil Beaumont's store, way out here in the middle of no place. At least, there was a logical explanation for that. She was probably up for the same job at Henderson that he was. A bit odd, that, as their talents—skill sets, she would have called them—lay in very different areas. But they were both übercompetent, as any headhunter would have to know. Still, what were the chances that she'd end up at that country store, needing a ride in one of the mountains' worst storms of the season just as he pulled in? Fate was trying to tell them something, and he, for one, was listening.

The fact that she'd end up staying with him in an isolated cabin fell into a different category of unlikelihood. Impossibility, more like. And yet, there she sat in the bucket seat next to him, staring out at the snow as if it held some message.

Laura Barber, the shy thing who'd turned into a wild

woman one night, nearly dragging him into an empty bedroom at the end-of-semester party. The woman who'd promised sex so uninhibitedly; she'd singed the edges of his imagination. The woman who never spoke up in class but who'd whispered filthy words in his ear while she'd unfastened his belt and started in on the zipper of his slacks. Unfortunately, she'd given off enough clues of her intoxicated state to keep him from following through, just barely managing to stop things before they'd gone too far.

Laura Barber . . . the one who got away. Hell, the one he'd let get away. Damn his conscience all to hell.

"Do you own this truck?" she asked after several minutes of silence.

"Rented."

"Do you always drive something so big?"

Right. The queen of green. "What were you driving?"

"A hybrid."

"If you'd had one of these, you wouldn't have gone off the road."

"Touché." She looked him in the eyes for probably the first time since she'd climbed aboard. "Truce?"

"Sure." Although, how he'd manage that would take some mental gymnastics. She wore the same scent she had all through business school. Nothing exotic, just kind of clean and sweet. She'd wrapped the scent around him that night. It still went straight to his gut, and now, he had the mother of all hard-ons. Truce, indeed.

He stared out the windshield. "That your hybrid up ahead?"

She squinted, peering forward. "It is."

He pulled up beside the car, set the brake, and pushed the gear lever to park. "Leave the engine running for heat. Give me your keys."

"I can get my bag myself."

He held out his hand. "I thought we had a truce."

After fishing in her purse, she produced a key on rental company chain and handed it over. Now, he could get away from her perfume for a few seconds. Maybe the cold would do something to ease his boner too.

He climbed out of the truck and shut the door behind him. His boots sinking into snow halfway to his knees, he trudged the few feet to the hybrid and used the key to open the trunk. She traveled light—just one carry-on and a suit bag. If he looked inside, which he wouldn't, he'd no doubt find a formless skirt and jacket combination. She could almost, but not quite, hide her plush figure under all the layers of clothing she wore.

After closing the trunk, he scrambled back to the truck and stowed her things in the back. Then, he took his seat in front and set the gear to low to take them down the snow-covered highway.

"You seem to know your way around," she said.

"I grew up near here."

"You look the part. All you need is a Stetson." She actually smiled. Not much but enough to curve that tempting lower lip. No matter how hard she tried to blend into the woodwork, that mouth and her enormous brown eyes kept her from pulling it off. Great, now he was thinking about her mouth.

"What are you doing in these parts?" he asked, even though he had a pretty good idea of the answer.

"Job interview," she answered.

"Henderson?"

"How did you know?"

"My interview is day after tomorrow," he said. "Doesn't look as if either of us is going to make it."

She groaned. "Oh no."

"Don't worry. You still have a chance."

"Why wouldn't I?" she said. "They'll understand about the storm."

"I didn't mean that. I meant the competition."

"What . . . oh." She glared at him. "You don't think I can beat you for the job."

He didn't answer but only smiled.

"Competitive to the end, eh?" she said.

"Pot . . . kettle."

"Is this your idea of a truce?"

"Sorry. Force of habit." He turned the truck off the main highway onto the narrow road that led to Jeff's cabin. Here, even the four-wheel drive wouldn't help them if he made a bad move. He'd have to concentrate on something besides the chaos in his jeans. The heavy vehicle inched along while the wipers slap-slapped against the windshield and the wind howled outside, swirling the snow around them. Laura sat huddled in the corner, her arms wrapped around her ribs.

"Frightened?" he asked.

She bit her lower lip. Even a short glimpse of that out

of the corner of his eye put his mind in places where it didn't belong.

"A little," she said after a moment.

"I'll take care of you." Boy, howdy, would he. *Stop it, damn it. Now.*

Normally, she'd have bristled at any suggestion that she needed help with anything. She must have been really scared not to say a word but just sit there, making herself small. If he weren't careful, she'd start tugging at his protective instincts. But then, when had he ever been careful where a woman was concerned? Well, maybe once . . . with this woman.

"Is it much farther?" she asked.

"A few more yards." Of course, in a storm in the mountains, a few more yards could stretch on forever. How had the pioneers ever managed?

The cabin came up on him unexpectedly. He must have misjudged how far they'd come because the outline of the building appeared directly ahead of them before he'd realized they'd arrived. He let a breath out slowly, and his shoulders relaxed. Though he'd never admit it to Laura, navigating under these conditions was a bit of a crapshoot, and he hadn't felt all that comfortable himself.

He steered the truck into the carport and cut the engine. When he turned off the headlights, they fell into darkness for a moment. All the better for him to sense the woman next to him. Her scent and the sound of her breathing filled the space around him. It was going to be an interesting few days.

If THE CABIN had appeared rustic from the outside, the interior somehow managed romantic and high-tech at the same time. Laura left her ruined shoes in the enclosed entryway, what Ethan referred to as a "mini mudroom," and followed him into the main living area. When he hit the switch, lights came on around the baseboards, producing enough illumination to suggest the interior of an elegant restaurant.

"Solar power?" she asked as she tipped up her carry-on and draped the suit bag over it.

"From batteries beneath the house," he said. "The system gives off heat as well as light."

"And the heat rises to fill the room."

"Once I get the woodstove and a fire going, we'll be toasty."

"Nice." They'd been bandying that word around a lot. This time, it didn't carry extra meaning.

Ethan put the bag of groceries on the counter in the kitchenette. "Settle in."

She glanced around. "Are there other rooms?"

"Bathroom."

"Then, where would you like me to settle in?"

He paused in the act of stowing a carton of eggs in the refrigerator. After a moment, he straightened, placed his elbow on the door and assumed his too-casual pose again. "You take the sleeping loft. I'll camp out on the couch."

She checked the piece of furniture in question. "Is it big enough for you?"

"I'll fold into it."

"Because, I don't really have to—"

"Take the loft. As you observed, heat rises. You'll be comfortable up there."

The baseboard heating was having an effect on the temperature, but not enough for her to remove her coat.

"I'll lay a fire," she said.

"You know how to do that?"

"It's not rocket science."

"Be my guest."

While he continued putting away groceries, she went to the huge stone fireplace and knelt to check out the supplies. Plenty of wood and kindling. Starting with crumpled newspaper, she built what should soon be a good blaze. She found matches, lit the paper, and sat back on her heels to watch the fuel catch.

Out of nowhere, a male hand appeared in front of her, holding a glass of red wine. She took it and glanced up at the towering figure of Ethan Gould. "Thanks."

"I didn't know for sure if you'd want anything to drink."

"I'm good with wine. It's tequila I need to stay away from." Damn it, why had she said that? She shouldn't have mentioned anything that could remind him of that night. Or remind herself, for that matter. She sipped some of her drink and stared into the fire.

Of course, he didn't do the easy thing and go back to the kitchenette and leave her alone with the memory. Oh no, he had to sit down beside her in front of the fire.

"Want to talk about the two-ton elephant in the room?" he asked.

"No."

"I do."

"Fine," she said. "You talk. I'll listen."

"Doesn't work that way."

"Look, Ethan." She took a fortifying sip of her wine and let it roll around on her tongue. He had good taste, she'd give him that. Eventually, she had to face him. When she did, she somehow ended up lost in the reflection of the fire in his eyes.

"Laura . . ." he prompted.

"I wasn't myself that night." Lord, how embarrassing. If he wanted to talk about this, why didn't he say something or do something? Why was he putting it all on her? "I behaved inappropriately toward you."

He gave her a lopsided smile. "Is that what they're calling it now?"

"Please. You'll make me blush."

"So what?" he said. "No one's ever died of blushing."

She could. Her heart fluttered in her chest, and her stomach felt full of cold lead. When her hands trembled, she set her glass on the hearth rather than spill red wine on the carpet.

"Hey, hey." He put his glass next to hers and took her hands in his. "It's not that serious."

When she couldn't take any more gazing into his eyes, she switched to staring at the fire. "You could probably have sued me for harassment."

"Harassment?" he repeated. "How do you figure that?"

"You obviously didn't welcome . . . um, return feel the same . . ."

"Because I didn't follow through?"

She clenched her teeth together and sat in utter, silent shame.

"You'd had too much to drink, Laura," he said. "Only a bastard takes advantage like that."

"Well," she pulled her hands from his and took a steadying breath. "It was a long time ago. I'm glad we settled it."

"I don't call that settled," he said.

She stared into the fire again. If she didn't look at him, maybe he'd go away. "I do."

"Damn it, Laura, you're going to deal with this." Taking her chin in his hand, he turned her head until she had to look at him. "Do you know how exciting you were that night?"

"I was drunk and disorderly." Drunk enough for him to have rejected her but not enough for her to have forgotten all the things she'd said to him. No one on earth had ever heard of her fantasies, but after that encounter, this man had.

"You turned me on like crazy," he said. "I went nuts trying to figure out how to get you to make the same invitation sober."

"It was a long time ago, Ethan."

"I would have called you, but I figured that would have embarrassed you."

"I'm glad you didn't."

"I kept putting myself in places where I'd bump into you by accident, but you disappeared"—he gestured with both hands—"poof."

"I don't want to talk about this," she said. "You promised."

He studied her for a long moment before picking up his wine again. "Yeah, I guess I did."

"Thanks for understanding." This time, when she lifted her glass, it didn't wobble.

"You'll at least eat dinner with me, I hope."

"Of course," she said. "This is excellent wine, by the way."

"It should go with the steaks. How do you like yours?"

"Rare."

"Rare it is." With the knuckle of his free hand, he tapped the end of her nose before rising and sauntering back to the stove.

She took a deep breath—the first truly relaxing one she'd had since he strolled into the country store—and watched him rinse vegetables for salad in the sink. She ought to help him, but he seemed to know what he was about. Besides, the world was a safer place with distance between them.

So, he'd refused her that night out of gallantry. Or so he said. That made things marginally less humiliating. Sort of.

As he worked on their dinner, his movement fluid as he went from counter to refrigerator to cabinet and back, she couldn't erase the memory of that lean body against hers. The kisses . . . sweeter and more potent than the margaritas that had caused her to lose control. And the misery, the soul-crushing disappointment, when he'd pushed her away.

Now that they'd discussed the two-ton elephant, the whole incident was closed. Over and dealt with. Finito. Somehow, that made her stomach only queasier.

Chapter Two

"LAURA, MOVE OVER."

Asleep. Dreaming. Someone was telling her to move over. The salesman in her mind's eye who was trying to sell her the huge purple SUV with the tiny tires. Why would he want her to move over?

"Come on, Laura. Please."

She opened her eyes to a strange place with a low ceiling just visible above her. The loft. The cabin. A hand shook her arm.

"Ethan?" she asked. "What's wrong?"

"I'm freezing. Move over."

She clutched the covers to her chest and turned. The floorboard lighting cast enough illumination to show to his face at the top of the ladder, less than a foot from hers. "What happened?"

"The fire went out."

"You should have kept it going."

"I was asleep, okay?" He climbed the last few rungs and lifted the covers so he could slide in beside her.

"What are you doing?"

"This is the only warm spot in the cabin."

She retreated toward the back of the loft, but that didn't take her very far away from him. "The wood stove."

"It sends all the warmth up here," he said. "Heat rises, remember?"

"But you can't—" Before she could get another word out, he pressed his foot against her leg. Even through her pajamas, it felt like ice.

"Hey!" she cried.

"See what I mean?" he said. "Have pity. You don't want me to freeze my butt off, do you?"

"Heaven forbid." He had a glorious ass, just like every other part of him. Not that she'd ever stared at it or anything.

"Thanks." He pulled the covers up under his chin and settled back. At least, they had two pillows so they wouldn't have to share. But how was she supposed to sleep with him taking up all this room with his scent and his, well, maleness? Maybe a little small talk would make things less tense.

"That was a great dinner. You're a good cook," she said.

"Steak and salad's easy."

"But zabaglione? That takes some skill."

He shrugged, his shoulder brushing hers. "Glad we found the marsala. Jeff keeps a stocked liquor cabinet."

"I noticed."

"Maybe I'll make you a margarita while we're here."

So much for small talk. "Ethan, don't."

"Laura, I . . ." He rolled toward her and something very solid pressed against her hip. Hard, male, and very large. He flopped onto his back again, and they lay in silence for a while.

"I guess you must have felt—" he said.

"Yeah."

"Sorry about that."

"Don't be. It's a natural male reaction," she said. Natural and about as awkward as anything natural could be. "Men get, well, hard all the time, don't they? At least, that's what I've heard."

Oh God, here they went again. The two of them together were some kind catastrophe waiting to happen.

"Are you kidding?" he asked. "You think this is some kind of random, meaningless event?"

"I think I don't want to have to talk about another elephant in six years." She rolled over, pinning herself against the wall with her back to him. "Good night, Ethan."

"Oh no you don't." He caught her shoulder and pulled her back against the mattress. "We're going to take care of this right now."

"For heaven's sake, there's nothing to take care of."

"My anatomy disagrees."

"I don't know anything about anatomy. I was a business major."

"Gee . . . hosophat." He propped himself up on one elbow and waved his finger under her nose. For a moment, he looked ready to deliver a lecture, but then, his expression change, turning serious, and he stared at her mouth.

All the air whooshed out of the tiny space, and she parted her lips to try to breathe. As soon as she had, he moaned and closed the distance to place his lips over hers.

She absolutely melted under the sweetness of his kiss. Better even than her memories of the ones she'd had before, and those had grown more and more heated over the years. His mouth moved with enough pressure to command a response from hers. And she responded. How could she not? She answered with her own lips, exploring every curve, every bend of his mouth. Soon, the sounds of their breathing filled her ears. Harsh and labored. Two people becoming aroused. When his tongue grazed her lower lip, she had to push him away to drag air into her lungs.

"What are we doing?" she whispered.

"What we should have done six years ago."

"Oh God."

"Praying won't do you any good, lady. This is going to happen. Answer one question first."

She stared at him. That question might spare her if she came up with the right answer. On the other hand, did she really want to be spared? She'd desired him that night six years ago. That hadn't changed.

"What?" she said.

"Protection," he said. "I have only one condom in my wallet."

"I'm on the pill." Damn it all, why had she told him that? She'd only kissed him. She hadn't agreed to go any further than that. She could have lied and ended this. Now she'd given him permission.

His grin said the meaning of her confession had registered. "Sweet, sexy Laura. As cautious as ever."

"This is crazy, Ethan. It didn't work six years ago, and it won't now."

"I didn't enjoy pushing you away, Laura." His voice came out deep, lusty. "I wanted to bury myself inside you. I still do."

"I don't know. It's . . ." *complicated.* Only, it wasn't, at least not as far as her body was concerned. Her body was finding things very simple, indeed.

"We're business people. We negotiate all the time," he said. "We'll make a deal."

"What kind of deal?"

"Give me the time we have here. A few days until the tow trucks show up. Once we leave this cabin, I'll never bring this or six years up again."

"What do you get, aside from the obvious?"

"I want everything you promised me six years ago," he said. "All of it."

What temptation. With the help of some good Mexican liquor, she'd laid everything on the table. Everything she'd ever wanted to do with a man's body. All of it involving the erection she'd felt against her hip a few moments ago.

All her adult life, men's bodies had fascinated her, but she'd experienced only vanilla sex. Under covers, in the dark. If she took his deal, she could play with his big beauty—feel it stiffen, watch it climax, and then get it erect again. She could tease it and lick it until he couldn't stand any more, and then she could mount him and ride him the way she'd done in daydreams since the first day she'd laid eyes on him.

"Think about it. No inhibitions. No 'it's naughty.' And I do *not* want to hear the word 'inappropriate,' " he said. "And then, we can leave all that behind here. I'll never say a word about it again or that party, either."

"You promise?

"That's the deal."

Talk about an offer she couldn't refuse. Hot, kinky sex for days. His sex in her hands, in her mouth, inside her body. Any way she wanted it. Maybe even the one fantasy she hardly let herself dwell on. Then, she could walk away guilt-free, knowing neither of them would speak about this ever again. She could put her involvement with this man where it belonged . . . in the past.

"Okay." She stuck out her hand to shake.

"Oh no," he said. "I can think of a much better way to close this deal than that."

Then, he launched a full-blown, multiflank assault on her senses. He kissed her again, but this time, his body covered hers as he stole her breath with his mouth. Heat rose, for sure. Already the small space of the loft had warmed to the point where she didn't need blankets. The man had to have a furnace inside him because his skin heated hers wherever they touched.

When even lips weren't enough, she probed with her tongue in search for his. When she found it, a current of need shot through her, downward past her heart all the way to the secret place between her legs. How did he manage to arouse her so easily? She'd known a few men, but none of them had moved her like this.

After a bit, he lifted his face from hers and gazed down at her. In the dim light, she could just make out the haze of arousal in his eyes. He really did want her.

"You're amazing," he whispered.

"Just don't stop."

"Not a chance." He dipped beneath her chin to nibble at the sensitive flesh of her throat. All the while, his fingers worked the buttons of her pajama top until he'd parted the sides to expose her breasts. Even that didn't chill her, but then, he covered one with his hand while taking the other nipple into his mouth.

Sucking in a breath with a hiss, she arched her back. So intense. Unbelievable.

He released her. "Did I hurt you?"

"I told you not to stop," she said, pounding on his back. "You stupid man."

"That's my girl." He chuckled and went back to work. This time, he performed his magic on the other breast, the heat and moisture of his mouth tugging at the peak. It had already tightened to a hard nub, and now, he teased it until she couldn't contain a whimper. He'd set a fire inside her that burned from the inside out. Her sex clenched. Empty now and craving him. He'd fix that soon. He'd take that glorious hardness and fill her with it. Already, she'd grown wet, soaking the lips of her sex. She might be embarrassed about that if he hadn't made her so insanely aroused.

"I want you naked," she said, hardly recognizing her own voice. That was the sound of a woman with demands. A woman who didn't give a fig for anything but her own needs. She didn't have to. She could enjoy this man any way she wanted and then never have to face him again. She could excite him any time she wanted and enjoy the consequences.

With her new boldness, she flipped them over and pushed his T-shirt over his ribs and shoulders. As soon as he'd yanked it over his head and tossed it God knew where, she feasted on him. After laying kisses along the angle of his jaw, she trailed her tongue down his throat and dipped it into the hollow above his collarbone. Her breasts pressed against the firm muscles of his chest, creating even more stimulation for the hardened tips.

Slithering lower, she ground her body against his while she teased his male nipples with her thumbs. His hardness pushed against her belly, even larger than she'd remembered. She ought to fear a monster like that. It could hurt if he weren't careful. He wouldn't let that happen. The man who'd refused to take advantage of her six years earlier wouldn't harm her.

Rolling onto her side, she snaked her hand between their bodies to measure his dimensions with her hand. In response, he trembled.

"Easy, tiger," he said.

"Let me feel you."

"I've wanted you a long time. I'm working with a hair trigger here."

"You said whatever came into my mind," she said. "Naked. Now."

Lifting his hips, he pushed the pajama bottoms down and then squirmed out of them. Now, she could touch him directly, circle her fingers around his girth, and rub the velvet tip of him with her palm. His hand closed over hers, stilling its movement.

"You can explore some other time, okay?" he said. "I seriously need to get inside you."

"Oh yes," she whispered.

"First, I'm going to make you ready."

Whatever that involved, it sounded good. She lay back and let him run his big hand over her body to the waistband of her pajamas. When he pushed it downward, she helped him remove the last bit of clothing that separated them. Now, he stretched out beside her, propped up on his elbow while his fingers went to the lips of her sex.

"You're already wet, baby," he murmured.

Burying her nose in his shoulder, she did her best to hide her face.

"That's a good thing," he said. "It makes me proud you want me so much."

"I do."

"Look at me while I touch you," he said.

"Can't."

"Sure, you can. Try it."

His finger landed on her most sensitive flesh, sending a current of fire through her sex. Her body jerked, and she found herself staring up into his face. He still wore the lazy smile of an aroused male.

"That's the spot, huh?" he said.

"Ethan." His name came out half a plea for mercy and the other half begging for more.

He touched her again, stroking gently. "You're hard."

"Yes, yes." Now, she could only surrender. Shyness no longer mattered. Her imperfections didn't count for anything. Even the fact that he wanted her retreated to the back of her mind somewhere. Nothing existed except for the movements of his finger. The flicking and rolling and . . . oh! . . . the constant press, press, press.

"Hot. Sweet." He dipped his finger inside her. It made a wet sound coming out, and then he went back to rubbing her in a maddening rhythm that promised to push her past the boundary but never quite got there.

"Please," she moaned. "Please. I need . . ."

"Ready for me?"

"God, yes. Now."

"I thought you'd never ask." He positioned himself between her legs. Now, instead of his fingers, the smooth head of his shaft slid between her folds. When the time came, it took no effort to accept his bulk as he slid easily into her. When he'd embedded himself fully, he held himself still over her, supported on his upper arms.

"Baby, you feel good."

She couldn't have spoken to save her life. She could breathe in only shallow puffs of air against his neck. No man had ever filled her so completely, owned her body so totally with his own.

Then, to top that miracle, he moved inside her—a slow surge and retreat that stroked her inner walls. In total bliss overload, she closed her eyes, shutting out everything but him. His scent, the stroke of his skin against hers, the passage of his sex inside her.

"Ah, damn," he breathed. "Too good."

She let her hands drift over his back, downward to where his muscles bunched to create those amazing thrusts. He moved faster now, going deeper and harder.

"Not going to last," he said. "Make it up to you."

Oh no. The mere thought that he might leave her was too much. That he could create this heaven and then take it away from her. She wrapped her legs around him, holding him against her. That made him even more frantic, his thrusting almost violent. It also brought him slamming against her hot button, and suddenly "not going to last" made all the sense in the world. The earlier fire he'd built came back even stronger. The flames licked at her, creating a buzzing, sparkling spiral inside her.

Finally, she snapped, and the world exploded into shards of brilliance behind her eyelids. Her sex seized on him and then broke into powerful spasms. She sobbed and then cried out at its force.

He stayed with her through the whole eruption and then roared as he pounded into her a few more times and stiffened in her arms. Inside her sex, he'd be spilling his lust. She could only pray that it was half as good as what he'd given her.

Finally, moaning, he rolled off her, pulling her with him so that they lay side by side in each other's arms. After tucking her head under his chin, he stroked her hair from her face.

"Ethan," she said.

"Hmm?"

"We're going to get cold if we don't pull the covers up."

"I know," he said, as he took a deep breath. "In a minute."

"Ethan."

"Hmm?"

"Was it . . ." She pressed a kiss to his chest rather than finish her question.

"Good?" he said. "Baby, you know it was."

She didn't say anything but lay, listening to his heart.

"Don't you?" he said.

"Sure." Why had she even asked the stupid question? She sat up, fumbled for the covers, and tugged them up to cover both of their bodies.

He pulled back and looked into her eyes. "Laura, when a woman has an orgasm like that, it makes a guy feel like a superstud."

"I was asking about yours."

"It took the top of my head off."

Her innards felt all warm and runny for a minute. "I'm glad."

"Don't ever worry about satisfying me," he said. "That is not going to be a problem."

"I'm *really* glad," she said and wormed her way back into his arms again, burying her face into the furrow between his pecs.

"I hope that tow truck takes a long time getting here," he said. "We have a lot of work to do on you, and I'm going to love every minute of it."

Chapter Three

ETHAN CHECKED THE oven for probably the tenth time. What in hell was he worried about? Everything would stay warm, and the pancakes wouldn't dry out unless Laura slept past noon. Only what kind of human being didn't wake up to the smell of bacon frying?

He ought to give up trying to kid himself. He didn't have a breakfast-is-getting-cold problem. He had a missing-Laura problem. Every minute seemed like an hour that he couldn't wrap his arms around her and kiss her and look into those gorgeous brown eyes. Thank God he'd thought to let the fire go out the night before.

Why in hell wouldn't she wake up?

He poured himself a second mug of coffee and went to the floor-to-ceiling windows to stare out at the landscape. Snow covered everything. It even climbed so high up the pines that the lower branches met the piles on the ground, weighed down as they were by piles of white of their own. It looked magical.

If he were a romantic kind of guy, he'd probably think up some comparison with a fairy tale or something. The princess isolated in her palace until the knight came to save her. Thank heaven, he wasn't prone to that kind of silliness.

Glancing up at the loft yet again accomplished nothing, so he cleared his throat loudly. When that didn't produce results, he went to directly below where Laura still slept on and coughed a few times. Finally, something moved up there, and her head appeared over the edge.

"Morning, sleepy head," he called.

She looked tousled and slightly disoriented, her eyes not focusing completely. She rubbed her face. "Wow, did I sleep."

"I noticed."

"Is that coffee?"

"What else?" he asked, lifting his mug. "French roast."

"I'll be right down."

"I put Jeff's robe up there for you." Fewer layers and easier to open than her pajamas. Heaven help him if she put both on. He'd scorned anything more than a robe himself, and for the same reason. Easier to strip.

He smiled as he went back into the kitchen, allowing her to come down on her own. The eagerness for her ought to come as no surprise. He'd thought about her for six years, dragging out the memories to torment himself with what-ifs. What if he'd let her succeed in undoing his fly and taking out his cock?

Would she have dropped to her knees to suck on the head and then slide her lips down the shaft? Would she have gotten him so hot he'd have to make a burrow for them under all the coats and jackets on the bed so that he could fuck her brains out with their whole graduating class just down the hall? Would she have come like a rocket taking off and blast him into the stratosphere with her?

Now he knew the answers. Yes yes yes. Not only that, but she was even better than he'd imagined.

As he got the food out of the oven and took it to the table he'd already set, the soft sound of footfalls came up behind him.

"Just look at that," she said.

He turned to discover she'd gone to the windows and was gazing wide-eyed at the snowscape.

"Good thing we didn't end up stuck in it," he said.

"It's beautiful."

"Jeff has snowshoes. We can tromp around outside if you have warm clothing."

"I'll find something." She went to her bag and got out a small travel case. "Breakfast smells great. Let me just wash up."

He nodded and watched as she went to the bathroom. She hadn't bothered with her pj's, and there wasn't anything else in there for her to put on. He'd have her seminaked when she came back out. His plan was working. As soon as he'd eaten breakfast, he'd get some dessert. If he got through breakfast without his member giving his intentions away.

While she did what women did in the bathroom first thing in the morning, he finished setting the table. He'd put it by the double-paned windows so that they could bask in the warm sunlight and stare out at the beauty of the snow-covered mountains in the distance. He didn't have flowers or cloth napkins, but he did pour the maple syrup into a small pitcher. Once he'd set out the coffee carafe, everything looked pretty good.

Not as good as Laura did, though. When she came back, she gave him a shy smile. It curved her lips in a particularly delicious way, so as soon as he had her seated, pushing in her chair for her, he took his own place across from her. The table could hide his member because the lesson he was about to give her, for sure, was going to make him stiff.

He piled some pancakes on her plate and then served himself. Furrowing her brow, she looked down at the generous helping he'd given her. "After that huge steak last night, you expect me to eat all that?"

"If it tastes good," he said. "I want you to enjoy yourself in every physical way possible."

"I'll blow up like a balloon."

To make his point, he slid several slices of bacon from the platter onto her plate. "We're going to be here for only a few days."

"I'll have to spend hours in the gym to work it all off."

"Women. Half of you want to look like porn stars," he said. "And the other half want to look like sticks."

"You know porn stars?"

He stopped with his fork halfway to his mouth. "Did I say I did?"

"Then, how do you know what they look like?"

He didn't answer that dumb question, just stared back at her.

"Oh," she said.

"Don't tell me you've never watched an adult movie."

This time, she was the one who kept her mouth shut, but her cheeks flamed a hot pink.

"You're blushing again," he said.

"No one ever died of blushing, a wise man once said." She remembered. How touching.

"I think it's time we got you over some of your shyness," he said.

"How do you plan to do that?"

He stared into his coffee. "Let's practice talking dirty."

"Dirty, like . . . um . . . how?"

He glanced back up at her. "The way you talked to me before."

"I don't remember much," she said. "I was intoxicated at the time."

"Okay, we'll start from the beginning and go from there?" he said. "What do you call your privates?"

"Privates?" She hooted softly. "You call that talking dirty?"

"I want to know what you call that place between your legs."

She nibbled on her bottom lip for a moment. "It's my sex."

He hooted right back at her. "You call *that* talking dirty?"

"Okay, vulva. Vagina."

"That's medical, Laura. It's not dirty."

She leaned back and crossed her arms over her chest. "What do you call it?"

"Your pussy."

"That figures." She picked up her fork and shoved a big slice of pancakes into her mouth.

"Go ahead, say it," he said. "I dare you. Say 'my pussy.' "

She mumbled something around her food.

"Chew first," he said. "I'll wait."

Finally, she swallowed and then took a drink of her coffee. When she couldn't escape the inevitable any longer, she set her mug back down. "It's my pussy. Satisfied?"

Oh brother. "It's incredibly sexy when you put it that way."

"Come on. I said it all right?"

"All right. What did we do last night?"

She stared at him out of the corner of her eye. "We had sex."

"Bzzzt. Wrong."

"We didn't make love. It was a business deal."

Come to think of it, sex that good felt like making love to him, even if they weren't ever likely to use the *l* word in serious conversation.

"You must be able to think of another word."

"We balled. We screwed. We shtupped," she said.

"You're getting warmer."

Her eyes narrowed. "I know what you want me to say."

Leaning across the table, he stuck his nose as close to hers as he could. "So, say it."

"We fucked," she shouted. "Satisfied?"

"Oh yeah, baby. We fucked. And it satisfied me for a while." Not a whole lot longer though, because he was well on the way to requiring another good fucking.

She groaned. "You're impossible."

"So, what do you call the thing in my pants?" Or in his robe, in this case. Getting fully erect and sticking out of the gap between the halves.

"I don't suppose penis is the right answer."

"Only if you're my doctor."

"It's your member, your dick, your tool, your rod, your cock," she said. "Should I go on?"

"That's enough," he answered. "For now."

"I don't think I'm done, though. Now that you've unlocked my inhibitions, let me tell you what I'd like to do with your instrument."

"Knock yourself out."

"Well, Mr. Gould, what I'd like to do is suck on your cock."

He took a drink of his coffee, smiling at her over the rim. "Good girl."

"I'd like to swallow your dick, but there's probably too much of that, so maybe I'll just run my tongue around the head until you squirm."

She had a hidden talent for dirty talk, obviously. If he weren't already turned on in a major way, she'd accomplish that in no more than a few seconds. In a minute, he'd be bumping up against the underside of the table if she got any better.

"In fact, I'd like to nibble on you," she said. "Gently, of course. I wouldn't want to do any damage to that huge erection."

"I'd lay off exaggeration, if I were you," he said. "It makes the rest of your speech less believable."

"But it is huge." She stroked the saltshaker, running her fingers up and down the way she might pump his shaft. Either the sun coming through the windows had gotten warmer somehow, or she was making him seriously hot.

"You know what?" she went on, as she picked up the syrup pitcher. "I'd like to pour this all over you and suck it off."

"You want to pour that on my prick?"

"Prick," she declared. "I forgot that one."

"I'll remind you if you forget again."

"Prick," she repeated, rising from her chair with the pitcher still in her hand. "I'd like to use this to turn your prick into a lollipop."

His jaw dropped. "You're kidding, right?"

"Come on, Ethan, we both know you have major wood under the table."

"Major wood?" Great, now he was the one who sounded like an echo.

"I know all the words. I just don't use them." She bent over and placed an innocent kiss on his lips. "Now, be a good boy and turn your chair around."

Good Lord, she meant it. "That stuff is sticky."

"I'm going to lick it all off. If I miss any, we can take a shower together, and I'll wash you." She gave him a wicked grin. "I can lather you up and fondle you all the way down to your balls."

"I think I've been punked," he said. "You obviously know what you're doing."

"Are you going to turn around, or do I have to operate under the table?"

Put that way, his choice was obvious. If he didn't co-operate, he wouldn't get to watch her as her lips covered the tip of his cock and then slid down the shaft. She was going to give him a blow job, and if he had to put up with a little stickiness in the short hairs, so be it. Thank goodness he'd heated the pancakes, not the syrup.

Finally, he obeyed her order and turned his chair outward. She took one look at him and grinned.

"Ethan, Ethan," she said. "You're quite a man."

"It's not gentlemanly to brag."

"And you have so much to brag about." She knelt between his legs and pushed the two halves of his robe apart. His member had become fully erect minutes earlier. It seemed to realize it was about to get a treat, standing proudly—and very stiffly—away from his body.

She tipped the pitcher slowly until the syrup left in a narrow stream. It coated the tip of him and dribbled down the sides. Before it got too far, she set the pitcher on the top of the table and bent to slide her lips over him.

The glorious fucking the night before ought to have taken some of the edge off his lust. This was a whole different world of excitement as he watched her mouth slowly descend over his swollen cock. Even more, when she moved back up, she used a suction that drove his excitement into high gear.

Damn, but she was good. Over and over, she swallowed his erection and sucked him as if she couldn't get enough. Then she got really creative, as she'd promised. So gently it was a caress, she dragged her teeth along his shaft.

He almost shot out of the chair. "Holy shit!"

She stopped immediately. "Did I hurt you?"

"Hell no, you didn't hurt me," he said. "Where did you learn how to do that?"

"Just because I don't talk about these things doesn't mean I can't do them."

Her meaning somehow penetrated the fog of arousal in his brain. She meant she'd done this for another man. Maybe more than one man. If she did it this well, maybe she'd done it for dozens. Sweet, innocent Laura. The woman he'd denied himself because she'd had too many margaritas to know what she was doing. Maybe she *had* known what she'd been doing. Maybe she did it all the time. What a chump he'd been.

"What's wrong?" he said.

"Nothing."

"Nothing wrong with this guy." She pumped him a couple of times. Indeed, his cock's enthusiasm hadn't faded in the least. Clearly, his big brain couldn't solve any mental problems until his little brain had been satisfied.

"If everything's okay, I'll continue," she said.

"Everything's okay."

Way better than okay. Everything was splendid, just peachy. She went back to give him head better than anything he'd had in his hottest dreams. Up and down, her mouth moved. Swallow and suck as her hand worked at his shaft. He gripped the sides of his chair in his fists and watched through half-shut eyes as she performed his own, personal adult video at the breakfast table. Only this wasn't fake. It was real. Laura was loving his cock with enthusiasm that warmed his heart and made his brain feel as if it would explode.

Only the explosion wouldn't happen there. Soon, he'd lose the ability to hold back. In another minute or two, he'd come. He'd have to stop her before then. No ugly surprises for Laura.

At that exact second, she feathered the fingers of her free hand over his sac. He growled. No other way to describe it. "You'd better stop."

"Really?" She kept pumping with her fist and rubbed the head of his cock with her thumb. "I'm enjoying myself."

"But, baby . . . oh God."

"Just a little bit longer." She resumed the suction of her mouth on him as the wave swelled and crested inside him.

"Laura, stop!"

Finally, she had the good sense to obey. Before she could get up and get away from him, before he knew himself what he was doing, he'd hoisted her up and lowered her onto her back on the floor. Her robe fell open, and so did her legs, thank heaven. In seconds, he'd found his position between them and driven himself home inside her. He immediately set to thrusting into her. Savagely. The stubborn woman had given him no choice.

"Damn it, Laura, when a guy tells you to stop, do it."

"Don't *you* dare stop, or I'll have to kill you," she said.

How did she do this to him? Normally, he took things slowly, making sure the woman was wild for him even before he went to third base. All he did was touch this one, and poof. Or bang, in this case.

Wrapping her legs around him, she lifted her pelvis to meet his thrusts. "Ethan, don't slow down."

Slow down? Not a fucking chance. Now unable to speak, he could answer with only his body, so he kept at her as if he could pin her to the floor with his cock.

"Now. Hard. Please!" she cried.

Hot damn, she was going to come. He could hang on for that. He gritted his teeth, fighting the tension building in his balls. Just another second and another and another.

Bless her, her orgasm arrived, her muscles clamping down on him. Then, they burst into spasms all around him, the pressure better than her mouth had been on him because it showed her pleasure. Now, he could give in to his own need. Past any control, he thrust a few more times before exploding in orgasm. Perfect. Absolutely perfect, their voices rising together. It lasted for long moments before he could give no more, and he collapsed onto her.

A gentleman didn't sink his whole weight on his partner, but she'd melted his bones, and he wasn't going to be moving any time soon. She had more strength than he did, obviously, because her hands went to his back, her fingers tracing little patterns over the skin. She should have shoved him off, but she let him stay, his cock still buried in her, heaven wrapped all around him.

After what felt like an hour but was probably a minute or two, he finally rolled off her. When he left her body, she whimpered as if she couldn't stand being parted. Amazing woman. Lusty woman. How was he ever going to make love to someone else after having this?

LAURA SMILED TO herself as she trudged through, or rather over, the snow, Ethan panting as he brought up the rear. Maybe he could catch a breath if he stopped pestering her.

"You're being very annoying," he said.

"I am? That's rich."

"It's a simple question."

Perhaps, but the fact that he wouldn't let it drop said much more about him than it did about the "simple" question. "What was it again?"

"Where did you learn how to do that?"

She bit her lip to keep from laughing and stared straight ahead of her. "Do what?"

He caught her arm and turned her around. That took some doing given that she was wearing snowshoes, but she untwisted her body, lifting her feet until she faced him.

"Where did you learn to give head like that?"

"What do you mean 'where'?" she said. "Do you want to know the exact place?"

His jaw set into a rigid line. He wanted to know with whom she'd learned, of course, but he couldn't bring himself to admit it. In truth, she'd only imagined doing it, but she had watched a few adult films in her day, and they gave plenty of instruction. The rest she'd improvised, and the act had been even better than she'd hoped. Good enough to make her horny and wet for him, but she wasn't about to tell this arrogant male that and swell his ego even further.

"Have you . . . Did you . . . Jeez . . ." He put his hands on his hips and glanced around as if the snow might help him out of the problem he was causing himself. "Do that for other men?"

"I wasn't a virgin when you brought me here," she answered. "You probably noticed."

"Yeah, but did you do *that*?"

"I never used maple syrup before." All that was true in the strictest sense of the word.

"Oh, brother," he said.

Poor guy. She really ought to tell him the truth and end his misery. But a man with his reputation with women had no reason to be questioning her experience with sex.

"I used to think you were so shy and retiring," he said.

"I am."

"Now, I've created Laura Barber, the sex kitten."

She finally had to laugh at that, both at his discomfort

and the idea that anyone would think of her as a kitten of any kind. "That was our deal, wasn't it?"

"Yeah."

"Ethan, what's happened or will happen in the outside world has no existence here. For now, we own each other totally and exclusively. When we leave, it ends."

"You're right."

"Of course, I am," she said. "Now, spread your legs."

His eyes grew wide. "What are you going to do?"

"Nothing sex kittenish," she said.

"It's cold out here."

"Just, do it, big guy."

He lifted one snowshoe and moved it about a foot to the side. That allowed her to approach him and place one of her feet on the snow between his two and her other foot beside him. Finally, she stood close enough to run her arms up his back. "I gather you've never kissed while in showshoes before."

Circling his arms around her, he took her into a warm embrace. "I haven't."

"We're both virgins, then."

"I like the sound of that."

"Virgins?" she said.

"Kissing." His frown disappeared, finally, as he lowered his head toward hers. He'd kissed her before, but only as a prelude to coupling. This contact of lips felt more like comfort and sweetness. As his mouth moved over hers, it could have turned into something deeper, but it could also satisfy her without going any further. With the heat of exertion from tramping through the snow fading, his big body provided warmth and a haven of sorts. A place where she could come to snuggle and find safety.

He appeared to feel the same way because he made no move to get more intimate and no inclination to take her by the hand and lead her back to the cabin. He only ended the kiss and held her against him while he gazed down into her face.

Damn it all. What was she thinking? She'd seen the Gould charm from a distance. She ought to be able to detect it from this close. Pushing against his chest, she backed away a step. "I guess we know how to get close while wearing snowshoes now."

"Okay, what did I do wrong?"

"Did I say you did something wrong?"

"Your body said it," he said.

"Not much we can do in feet of snow and wearing all these clothes."

His brows furrowed. "I can hold you."

"Thanks. You did. It was really nice."

He glared at her for a moment. "Why do I feel as if I'm back in graduate school?"

"What's that supposed to mean?"

"You're giving me that look again."

Now, it was her turn to stare at him. "What look?"

"As if you don't quite approve of me."

"That's absurd."

"I wish I had a mirror so that I could show you your face."

He had a point; although, she wouldn't give him the

satisfaction of admitting it. He'd seemed to skate through things on his looks and ease with people. He could joke his way through class presentations, when she had to work for every graph, every point of logic, every phrase. Sure, his work was good, but he delivered it with an air that suggested he could knock off great presentations without breaking a sweat.

"You looked the same way when you saw me back in Phil's store," he said. "As if you were smelling something off."

"I was surprised to see you. Sex kitten stuff aside, I *am* shy. It isn't easy for me to interact with people I don't know well." She'd leave aside the question of whether coming on to him at that party counted as knowing him well. "People don't understand that. They think I don't like them when it isn't true."

"What's the rest of the world supposed to do with that? All we know is what you put out. If it's a 'buzz off' signal, we'll buzz off."

"Well, what about you? You seemed so damned competent, you make other people feel they don't measure up."

"That's not true."

"Name one thing you're not good at."

"Matrix algebra," he said. "I almost flunked that statistics class."

"We all had to struggle with that one. We had a study group. You should have joined it."

"I couldn't. You were running it."

He might have punched her in the gut. It hadn't come out mean. In fact, he looked embarrassed at having said it. "Explain."

"You scared me," he said. "A little."

"I couldn't scare anyone."

"You're so damned brilliant. We were all a little in awe of you."

What? She searched her memory for evidence that would prove or refute what he'd said. She'd had friends in graduate school. Not many but a few. The others had been more outgoing, but you expected that in a program that would lead to executive jobs. Most of the students expected to spend their professional lives dealing with people in one manner or another. Numbers people and analysts, like her, had their place, but they were different animals.

"You must have noticed that things got quiet when you spoke in class," he said. "We expected brilliance from your corner in the back, and you didn't disappoint."

"I didn't mean to put people off. I just didn't fit into social situations."

"Well, I'm glad we worked that out." He smiled again. It seemed more spontaneous now, not something he'd planned. "And I'm glad your hybrid went off the road."

"And you got to rescue me." Well, why not? No one would get through to Henderson because of the storm. The interview would wait for her. "Actually, I'm glad too."

"Great. Let me show you something."

He started off in front of her, lifting his feet in the awkward way the snowshoes required. She followed. Huffing along like this made a great workout. She wouldn't miss the gym while she was here. She'd appreciate his cooking too. What a great mini-vacation.

They went up a gentle rise, stopping at the top. The scene below took her breath away. They actually stood at the crest of a bluff with a valley below them and mountains in the distance. Everything was covered with pristine snow, except for a river that sparkled blue as it rushed over stones and curved through the valley floor.

He came up behind her, nudging his foot between hers so that he could get close enough to wrap his arms around her. "I love this place."

"I can see why."

"We should come back in the summer so you can see it when it's full of wildflowers."

Wrong. She'd come here out of necessity and had agreed to share only these few days with him. This wasn't the beginning of a Relationship with a capital R. When the snowplows came through, they'd go their separate ways. They'd understand each other better. They'd have memories. They were still competitors for the same job. One of them would get it, and they wouldn't see each other anymore. End of story.

Chapter Four

SEX WHENEVER YOU wanted it. What a concept. Laura slid the basket of French roast into the coffee maker and switched on the brew button. They had a couple of hours before dinner with no television or radio. She could read some annual reports, but with a human stud machine sitting only feet away from her, she somehow couldn't get her mind excited about bar graphs and spreadsheets.

The man had worked quite a transformation on her in less than twenty-four hours. She'd had always indulged cautiously, choosing men who were completely unrelated to her work and as concerned with discretion as she was. Sensible liaisons. Pleasant and casual—the exact opposite of sleeping with Ethan Gould.

Hell, not sleeping with. Fucking. She was fucking Ethan Gould. She'd fucked him in the loft and given him head at the breakfast table before fucking him again on the floor. It was a good word. She ought to use it more often.

So she did. "Fuck. Fuckety-fuck-fuck-fuck."

Ethan looked up from where he sat on the couch, reading an old sports magazine he'd found in the bathroom. "Something wrong?"

"Sensible liaisons are wrong," she said. "Fuck 'em."

He stared at her for a minute as if she'd started speaking Old Church Slavonic. "If you say so."

"I do. Sensible liaisons aren't worth"—What was that expression her brother used?—"a bucket of warm piss."

"Well now." His eyes flew open. "Alrighty then."

Maybe she'd gone a bit overboard with that one. Obscene was one thing, gross quite another. "I swear, you're making me crazy."

"Always happy to oblige. Anything I can do this minute to knock a few more screws loose?"

She bit her lip. "Probably."

He got up from the couch and headed toward the kitchenette. "Oh no, you don't."

"Don't what? I'm supposed to do whatever I want, aren't I?"

"Absolutely." He stopped just inches away from where she stood near the sink. "But you're supposed to tell me what you want so I don't have to guess."

"Are you ready again?"

"It's been hours, and I keep thinking of how your mouth looked on my cock," he said as he leaned closer. "And how much I want my tongue in your groove."

Her skin heated. He'd have to see the heightened color

on her cheeks. With any luck, he'd read that as excitement and not residual shyness. This whole fucking thing was still a bit new.

"Later," she said. "Right now, I want to do something else."

"Name it."

"A quickie," she said. "Fast and dirty."

"As if we rushed home for lunch and had only a few minutes."

A really naughty idea sprung into her head. How much fun to play out a scenario as someone completely uninhibited? That morning she'd allowed herself to talk dirty with him. This afternoon when could try acting the part.

"Not lunchtime," she said. "But a horny college student and . . . say . . . a plumber."

"A guy who's handy with tools." He tugged her close enough to show his tool was up to the job.

"Imagine I've been watching the sexy plumber work and getting hotter and hotter."

"Right, and I noticed the coed staring at me and got such a boner I thought I'd have to jerk off in my truck," he said. "I like the way your mind works."

She couldn't help but giggle out of pure joy. He offered anything she could want or need. She could have him anytime she asked for as long as they stayed in this cabin.

"Pretend we wasted half an hour while the plumber worked on the sink," she said. "So we have to act fast before my roommate gets home."

"You on the counter. My pants around my ankles," he said.

"Totally anonymous. Don't even kiss me. Just shove your cock in me and shake it around."

"Holy shit, Laura. I've created a monster."

"That's Miss Barber."

"I'm a full-service plumber, Miss Barber," he said. "Those slacks look kind of uncomfortable. Let me help you out of them."

He bent over and removed her loafers and socks. After pulling down the zipper of her pants, he tugged them and her panties down on one movement. Moisture followed along the inside of her thighs. When he had her legs free, he reached into her pussy hairs. "You have a major leak here, miss. It's oozing everywhere."

"Can you plug it for me?"

He straightened and undid his own fly. "I'll have to use the really big wrench."

"Hurry. It's getting worse." Damn, she was excited. Before this . . . before Ethan . . . becoming so damp and eager would have embarrassed her. She always grew wet enough to take a partner's member without pain. But her pussy had never begged so openly. She'd never admitted to a man that he'd turned her on so forcefully that orgasm wasn't optional but inevitable. She'd never have thought she could make herself vulnerable to Ethan again at all, but her body had taken that option away from her.

"Don't think I'm going to need any lube for this job," he said.

"Never mind that. We don't have time. Just put it in."

"Right." He lifted her until her butt rested on the edge of the sink and parted her legs. Then, he hesitated. Right on the verge of giving her all of him, down to the thick base, he stopped.

"Damn it, Ethan," she said. "What are you doing?"

"Counter's too tall."

What? After thinking up a nasty fantasy and deciding to act on it, after getting too excited to take the time to climb into the loft, they'd be stymied by the height of kitchen fixtures? "Well, shit. Think of something."

"Right." He sucked in a breath, let it out, and then took another. "I'll look in the cupboards."

He pulled out of her, leaving her balanced against the sink. She had to grab the edge to keep from falling off. His jeans still around his ankles, he fell to his knees and dragged things out of the lower cabinets. A roasting pan rattled against the floor, and pots flew. One top spun around and clattered downward. Eventually, he rose with one of those superheavy glass lasagna pans in his hand.

"Will that hold your weight?" she asked.

"It had better." He placed it upside-down on the floor and then stepped up onto it, almost tripping because of how his jeans bound his feet. After lurching a bit, he wrapped her legs around him and thrust into her.

"Yes!" she cried. Exactly what she'd needed. For a moment, she let the walls of her pussy absorb the shock of such fullness as she stared into his eyes. "Whatever you do, don't fall off."

"Hang on to the sink."

Still grasping the counter in her fists, she balanced her weight backward so that she could inch her pelvis toward his. In the bright afternoon light, she could actually watch his cock moving in her pussy. An amazing sight, the way their sexes had been created for each other. He was perfect—strong and beautiful and devoted to her pleasure. The pan beneath him rattled but held as he made pass after pass as deeply into her as she could take.

The coffee pot gurgled beside her, and her back bumped against the faucet on his deepest thrusts. Still, she could have wished the show to go on forever. It wouldn't, though. She was building to one hell of a crescendo. He must have sensed her nearness because he picked up the pace, risking life and limb, or at least a fall, to give her exactly what she needed. Hard and fast. Driving.

When her vision blurred, she closed her eyes and concentrated on the impending climax. Not much longer. Not much. "I'm going to come."

"Do it, baby."

"Fuck me, Ethan. I'm going to come!"

"I'm with you."

With a hard sink under her ass and the sounds of Ethan's rough breathing in her ears, she exploded into an orgasm that had her screaming. Then he was coming with her, his voice joining hers as he thrust into her and went rigid. As she gripped at him and he shot his semen into her, the two orgasms merged into one they could share. So pure, so complete.

Eventually, it had to end, and when it did, he pulled

her against him, her head on his shoulder. "Remind me to do all your plumbing, lady."

"God, yes."

"Another inhibition bites the dust?"

"Gone. Poof. Only . . ." As sanity returned, so did the reality of what they'd just done. She had to laugh. The whole thing was too absurd and too perfect. "I'll never look at lasagna the same way again."

He joined her, tipping his head back and roaring. "We're going to have to stay out of Italian restaurants."

That, of course, brought up the subject of whether they'd go to restaurants of any kind. That was not part of the bargain. But as she remembered the image of him crawling around on the floor with a massive hard-on, tossing aside pots and pans to find something exactly the right height, the idea of a life that included Ethan Gould didn't seem so remote or ridiculous as it had.

Maybe she'd come to like him. She'd certainly loosened up enough around him to ask for what she'd never dreamed of with another man. Maybe, just maybe, she'd come to trust him. Wouldn't that be something?

FINALLY THAT EVENING, Laura's moment of truth arrived. If Ethan hadn't kept talking about how turnabout was fair play, referring to the blow job she'd given him that morning, the lazy smile on his face would have told her what to expect. Their conversations earlier had led them into new territory. Tongue in groove, indeed. What would happen now would take them into a whole different dimension. Oral sex. She'd done it for him, and now he'd return the favor.

"Ready for another workout?" he asked as he sat beside her. From his place on the other side of her body, he didn't block the warmth from the blaze. Even a little thing like that spoke of his thoughtfulness. Was this truly the arrogant male she'd avoided all through graduate school?

"I don't know how I'm going to work out while I'm lying down."

"You don't?" One of his brows lifted. "I thought you were more imaginative than that."

"Something tells me you're going to explain the contradiction to me."

"I'm going to write a thesis on it. Right after I get my practicum done."

"Experimentation?" she asked. "I assume it's going to be hands-on."

"Hands and other body parts."

"Consider me your research volunteer."

He stretched out beside her, propped up on one elbow. He'd done that the night before, but in the dim light, shadows had hidden much of his face. Now with the light from the fireplace, she could look into his amber eyes, and bask in the glint of admiration in them. Admiration for her. Who would have thought that possible?

"You are so damned beautiful," he whispered.

"I was going to say the same thing about you."

"Me?" he asked, his eyes widened in surprise. "I do my best, but . . . beautiful?"

She reached up and trailed her fingers along the strong line of his jaw. "Beautiful."

When her hand neared his mouth, he dipped his head and caught her thumb between his lips. He sucked on it lightly for a moment. It wasn't a random action. She'd used her mouth that morning to give him pleasure—considerable pleasure if she'd read his reaction correctly. Now, he planned something similar for her. A slow ache blossomed between her thighs.

He'd probably laugh if she admitted that she'd never allowed a man to do that to her. Would she surrender to the ultimate intimacy with this man? Could she refuse without seeming hypocritical? Did she even want to refuse?

He took her hand and kissed each fingertip. "You got very quiet all of a sudden."

"That's me. Quiet."

"Quiet happy? Quiet sad? Talk to me, Laura."

She opened her arms. "I'd rather kiss you."

His eyes narrowed. "I don't know about that. I think you're trying to avoid something. You know my mind flies out the window when I touch you."

"That's the general idea, isn't it?"

"I think I'll torture you for the information." He trailed his hand over her belly and below. He didn't need to part her legs to slip his fingers between them as she'd already let them fall apart. He found her hot spot immediately, pressing through her slacks.

She sucked in a breath as the fire started inside her.

"Talk, Laura," he said.

"Later."

"Now." He touched her again, this time letting the pressure linger.

"You know what you're doing to me."

"I hope so."

She caught his wrist and lifted it. "I promise I'll tell you later. Fuck me now."

"You win." He bent down and took her lips in a kiss. This was no sweet caress like the one they'd shared after trudging through the snow. With a precision that would make a diamond cutter proud, he set about tasting every micro-millimeter of her mouth. He went to the corners and then the center, using his teeth to nip softly and his tongue to smooth his roughness over. Already, he'd stolen her breath, taking it as his own and giving it back.

More, oh more. No matter how much he gave, she couldn't get enough. Taking his face between her palms, she held him and answered. While their mouths tangled together, his hand went to the hem of her sweater. Easing it upward, he stroked her ribs and then cupped one breast. Even that gentle squeeze caused the nipple to tighten and grow stiff.

"Soft," he murmured against her mouth. "Perfect."

A day before, she would have protested that her breasts were too small to be called perfect. Now, they felt swollen and full, as if he could work miracles with her body. But then, perhaps he could.

He bent lower. Without removing her sweater completely, he unfastened the front clasps on her bra and took her nipple into his mouth. The night before, he'd done something similar. Today, she responded even more powerfully, as if he'd primed her body to react instantly. They knew each other now as lovers, and in a moment, she'd give up all shyness where this man was concerned.

Her mind drifted off to that special place where he wove a web of pleasure around her. Some other time, she'd have to make sure she gave as well as received. For now, she'd let him take control. He wouldn't disappoint her. If her mind didn't tell her that, her body did.

At his gentle urging, she sat up long enough to let him pull her sweater over her head and remove it and her bra. He took over undressing her, tugging her slacks over her already-bare feet and repeating the process with her panties. For a moment, he left her, and she lay, staring up at the beamed ceiling, while the fire warmed her skin. A log cracked and hissed, and a burst of light pierced the darkness. Then, Ethan returned, his body naked against hers, as he claimed her mouth again with his.

This kiss was prelude, yes, but it had its own identity, as though they could do no more than this all through the night. Twining her arms around him, she pulled him down onto her so that the firm planes of his chest rubbed against her nipples. As their lips tangled, withdrew, and sought each other again, her sex readied itself for the inevitable invasion. The lips felt swollen and heavy, and the slow ache inside her built to a steady throb. Still, she wouldn't rush this, not when she had a lover of such skill at her complete service.

As his lips left hers and traveled over her chin and below, his hands went on an exploration of their own. He

touched her in places she wouldn't have thought erotic—
her underarms, the space at the back of her knee, even
down to the arch of her foot. His mouth closed around
the breast he hadn't yet loved, and while he sucked that
nipple, his hand closed around the other—still moist
from his earlier caress. He kneaded the flesh and teased
the tip with his thumb, sending little zingers of excitement through along her nerves.

For these long moments, he owned her. If he stopped,
she would have wept with frustration. He wouldn't,
though. He'd continue driving her wild, and then, he'd
satisfy her. Though they'd been near-strangers when
they'd faced each other in that country store, they'd leave
here with the most intimate knowledge of each other.
He'd trusted her, and now, she'd trust him. No matter if
they never saw each other again, she'd always have this
night to savor. She'd always pull up the memories of this
fire with its flickering light and the pleasure of this man's
hands and mouth, playing her body like a finely tuned
instrument.

Lower still, he laid a trail of kisses between her breasts
and downward to her belly. Making his destination even
clearer, he pressed her legs apart and cupped her mound
with his hand. Just that pressure against her clitoris
started her on the climb to high arousal. She moaned, the
sound coming out harsh. No wonder. She had to struggle
for breath, fight to get air into her lungs. Another time
with another man, she might expect her lover to take her
now, and she would have been ready to accept him. Ethan
had a lot more planned for her. He'd as much as said so.

She'd settle in for a longer ascent—if, of course, she could make her sex wait.

He kept pressing, pressing with his hand as he moved lower. His body eased her legs farther apart as he settled between them. Finally in position with his face only inches from her sex, he parted the petals with his fingers and blew a hot breath over her hardened nub. The moment of truth lay only seconds away, and she couldn't help but tense. In her excitement, she'd already become wet. Would he find her repulsive? Was he doing this only out of a sense of obligation?

When his tongue touched her, she tensed further, stiffening. He stopped immediately and brought himself up to stare into her face. "Laura?"

Her skin flamed, and not only with arousal. She bit her lip and looked away.

He wasn't having any of that, obviously, because he caught her chin and forced her to return his gaze. "Hasn't anyone ever done this for you?"

"I wouldn't let them."

"Well, let me." The light of determination in his eyes said he wouldn't give up without a discussion. Besides, her shy nature couldn't keep her sex from making its own demands. She'd either have this man inside her soon or go crazy with unspent lust. Conversation was not an option.

He must have taken her silence as consent. In fact, it was. She'd let him take her to this border and past. He'd do it right.

So, when he resumed his place between her thighs and

again exposed her sex to his eyes and mouth, she touched his face in silent permission. And this time, when his tongue grazed her most sensitive flesh, she let the pure, animal delight of the caress rush through her, burning away all the fear and all the reservation.

What a revelation. What feeling. Such pleasure. How did you endure such a thing and come out on the other side? Stroke after maddening stroke, each pass of his tongue sent her further into a world of heartbeats and sighs and rising, blinding need. He acted as if he'd devour her, never getting enough. Reaching out, she found his hair and burrowed her fingers into it so that she could feel the movements of his head under her palm. If he found her moisture unpleasant, he gave no indication but lapped at her eagerly.

When she trembled and her hips refused to stay still, he grasped them and held her against his face. Her arousal grew to almost unbearable levels, her breath coming in gasps and now cries. The signs of impending orgasm came hot on each other. The building tension, the hypersensitivity of her bud, the feeling that she'd never get air again. If she could fight it off . . . just a few more second. Not yet. Not yet. Please.

Then, it was on her, and all choice disappeared. She let it take her upward into a place where nothing existed besides the clenching of her inner muscles and the cresting wave that broke over her.

She screamed, hardly hearing her own voice, as the contractions started and raced through her. Hard and fast, building on one another.

All through the storm, his tongue never slowed, as he urged the last fragment of response from her. He kept the heaven going until her body finally finished, and she sank against the carpet with a moan of utter completion.

When it had all ended except for the fluttering aftershocks in her sex, he scrambled up beside her and pulled her into his arms. Her face against his neck, and her hand against his chest, her fingers curled into a soft fist.

"Good?" he whispered.

"Oh . . ." *Breathe, breathe.* " . . . boy."

"Thanks for letting me be the first."

First, last, and always. No wait, that wasn't right. Something . . . to hell with it. She let him warm her in the front while the fire did its work against her back. If their heaven could truly exist on earth, this must be it.

They weren't done, though. The thick ridge of his arousal pressed against her belly said that clearly enough. She could have that too. And she could keep enjoying him for as long as they stayed here.

"You're an endless source of wonder, lady," he said.

"You're an endless invitation to ruin."

He laughed. "Have I ruined your reputation?"

"Absolutely," she answered. "I'll never be able to play ice queen again."

"You more or less blew that yourself six years ago."

She pushed away from him and stared into his face. "You didn't tell anyone, did you?"

"Of course, not. If I had enough scruples not to take advantage of you, I sure as hell wasn't going to brag to my buddies."

"Thank you."

"Besides, they all would have called me an idiot for not taking you up on your offer."

She could only stare at him. "They would?"

"No. Well, maybe some of them. You shouldn't take things so literally."

"How do I know how to take things?" she said. "I have no idea how men work."

"Beg to differ with you there," he said as he flexed his hips, pressing his erection into her flesh. "You know how I'm put together."

"I'm learning. What do you feel like doing with that thing?"

"Putting it inside you," he said. "I'll let you flesh out the details."

"As it were."

"As it were," he repeated. "You decide."

"Well . . ."

He kissed the tip of her nose. "Come on. No more shyness. We've gotten past that."

They had, indeed. She'd allowed him to give her the most intimate caress, and she'd not only survived it, she fairly glowed with joy and satisfaction.

Suddenly, a delicious image sprang, full-blown, into her imagination. Ethan lying on his back in front of the fire while she slowly impaled himself on his cock.

"I have it, but you'd better throw on a few more logs, first."

"That's quite a gleam in your eye."

"You'll enjoy it. I promise."

"Okay. Don't move from this spot." He sat up and moved the wire mesh screen away from the fire so that he could add more fuel. He needn't have worried that she'd leave him for even a second. She had the sexiest and best lover in the world. Where was she going to go?

After a bit, the added logs caught. A good thing, as the fire had dimmed and the room had become quite dark, and she wouldn't miss seeing what would happen next for all the tea in China. Now, she could watch his face as she sank onto him—see his eyes go unfocused and then close with delight. She'd catch every nuance of expression as his orgasm hit.

He turned back to her and lifted an eyebrow in question.

"Me on top," she said.

IF HE LIVED to be a hundred, Ethan would never get the image of Laura by firelight out of his mind. The flames gave her skin a warm glow as she parted the lips of her pussy and guided the tip of his member between them. Holding her hips, he helped her to go slowly so that he could watch her take him inch by inch. When she'd finished, their pelvises meeting, she let out a long, low breath and tipped her head back, her lips parted in an expression of pure bliss.

What a privilege to be able to do this for her. She honored him more than he deserved, but he'd accept anything she'd give him. He was only a man, after all, and when a goddess like her offered, you took.

"Warm enough up there?" he asked.

"Heat rises."

"It certainly does."

She groaned in a particularly delightful way. "You must have some kind of magic. I can't get enough."

"Take as much as you want. I'll make more."

"I believe you." Leaning forward, she placed her palms on his ribs and used the leverage to lift her hips up and then slide down to meet him again. The muscles inside her gripped him as she did, and he clenched his teeth to try to get some control. He absolutely would make this encounter last for as long as humanly possible.

"Did you get bigger?" she asked.

"I don't see how."

"Maybe it's the position." She repeated the up-and-down motions. "Oh God, yes."

Oh, baby. If she stroked his ego any harder, he wouldn't be able to get it through a doorway. She'd never been the type to flatter. If he could give her such intense pleasure, he must be doing something right. He'd do it over and over again for as long as she'd let him.

The realization changed things. He wasn't going to let her go when the plows came through. He couldn't say now where the two of them were headed, and he sure as hell wasn't going to figure it out with her riding his cock. They had some kind of future together, though. No one in his right mind gave up on a woman like this.

No, he'd have her again after they left here. Thank God for snowstorms and hybrids that ran off the road. Thank God for Jeff and this cabin. If anything different had happened, Laura Barber would be nothing more than a seduction that hadn't taken place six years earlier.

"Ethan?" she said.

"Yeah, baby."

"Does this feel as good to you?" she asked as she moved with a steady rhythm now, wiggling and squeezing him.

"It feels like heaven."

"I'm going to come again."

"You bet you are," he said. "I'm going to make sure you do."

"Make it last a long time."

"As long as I can."

"Good." She sat straight up now, and he took over thrusting. Still holding her hips, he pushed up into her in the same tempo she'd set. His control began a slow unraveling, but he needed to do this to make her happy.

It seemed to work because she cooed her approval and put her hands over her breasts to massage them.

Damn, what a vision she made. Her hair, which she normally kept tied at the nape of her neck, floated around her face, catching rays from the fire that turned the strands into different hues of gold and brown. Her beautiful, small breasts curved under the pressure of her hands, and the tips peeked out from between her fingers. And down below, her juices ran freely, sparkling droplets in the curls that covered her pussy. She was a goddess, all right, of love and lust and everything sensual. No man, other than he, would ever see her like this again.

"It's happening again," she cried.

"Let it come, baby."

Her orgasm would end him. He'd felt her contractions before and knew their power. When she finished, so would he. He could have her again tomorrow and beyond for as long as they continued to rock each other's worlds. He'd feel her come around his cock dozens, maybe hundreds of times, and each one would be as perfect as this would be.

By now, she moaned or whimpered on every passage of his cock, and he moved faster, driven by his need. Neither of them could wait any longer. Before he lost his head completely, he moved one of his hands to the place where he entered her and found her clit. As hard as it was when he'd taken it into his mouth. She was, indeed, close to the edge.

He massaged the little bud, rolling it and flicking his thumb against the tip. In response, she shuddered violently. Using his other hand, he kept her with him as his own movements became more out of control. He'd lost the option for gentleness long ago, and now he could only plow into her as the tension wound inside him.

"Yes!" she cried. "Oh yes, don't stop."

"Never."

She came, strong contractions coming one after another. The power of it shook him, sending his response into a new universe of arousal. His own orgasm started at the base of his spine and shot outward to every inch of his body. His sac tightened and sent a wave of liquid heat through him, finally shooting out of his cock and deep inside her. Even she must have felt it enter her. Then and then and then.

He shouted, his voice joining hers, as they climaxed together. In such perfect unison, such a miracle, such a joy. Even when it ended, the magic remained, spun all around them. She seemed to float down onto his chest even as her sex continued to grip him softly, a reminder of what she'd just given him.

He kissed the top of her head and stroked her shoulder, pulling a sigh from her as their heartbeats went back to normal.

He wasn't giving this woman up. As stubborn as she could be, he'd have to find some way to convince her. They had more days ahead of them than a few. That part was no longer open to negotiation.

Chapter Five

FUNNY THING ABOUT inhibitions. Once one fell, they all tumbled over like dominoes. But they left a residue of naughtiness powerful enough to create a more or less permanent state of sexual excitement. Luckily, Laura had the ultimate sex toy in Ethan Gould, and he'd given her permission to do anything with him that came to mind.

Now, on the afternoon of their second full day at the cabin, she sat on the couch studying him and letting her mind run wild with what she could do to him.

At the other end, he glanced up from his laptop and caught her staring at him. "Whoa, what's that look all about?"

"Look?"

"As if you'd like to eat me up," he said.

"Maybe I do."

He grinned. "Should I get the maple syrup out again?"

"I don't think I need the help." She eased closer to him,

took the laptop and placed it on the table at his elbow. "You know what I'd like to do?"

"I don't, but I'm pretty sure I'm going to enjoy it."

She put her lips to his ear. "I'd like to watch you come."

"Really?" He pulled back. "What about you?"

"I'm sure you'll take care of me later. I've never actually seen a man's cock ejaculate. It must be incredibly sexy."

"If you say so. I've never thought of it that way," he said.

"I have," she said. "A lot."

He gave her a lazy grin. "I'm at your disposal."

"Oh, I know." First, she needed to get him undressed. Kneeling in front of him, she bent to remove his shoes and socks. When she unzipped his fly, she found the outline of a semi-erect male member underneath his shorts. "Why, Ethan, you started without me."

"I can't seem to get completely soft with you around," he said. "You must give off some kind of pheromone."

She tugged at the waistband of his shorts, he lifted his hips, allowing her to pull them and his jeans off. He'd already grown thicker. It'd be fun to see how hard she could make him without actually touching him. More dirty talk, maybe. Telling him how much she wanted him and all the wicked things he did to her.

After getting back onto the couch, she removed his sweatshirt, easing it over his shoulders and head, and then dropped it to the floor.

"I'm in charge here," she said. "I want you to sit there, not touching yourself or me."

"Can I talk?"

"If you say the right things."

"Like what?"

"Like 'Laura, you make me so hot.' 'I'm going to come,' " she said. " 'Oh, baby.' That sort of thing."

He leaned toward her until his breath warmed her ear. "Oh, baby."

"Remember, no touching me. Just sit there and take what I dish out."

He put his hands by his sides and sat there smiling. Damn, but he was gorgeous. Sleek and finely muscled. Firm pecs gave way to a flat stomach. From there, a line of curling hairs led downward to where his cock had come to life.

She ran her palm over his chest. "You really made me crazy yesterday afternoon. I'd never had a man's mouth on my pussy before. My clit's getting hard now just remembering it."

"I can do that for you again," he said. "Any time."

"I'll take you up on that." Sure enough, his cock had stiffened. "Tell me, stud muffin, do you ever touch yourself?"

"Sometimes," he said. "Isn't it about time you touched me?"

"In a minute," she said. "Did you ever fantasize about me while you stroked your cock?"

He actually blushed. "For months after that party."

"What did I do in your fantasies?"

"Um." He paused for several seconds. "That's kind of embarrassing."

She lowered her hand to his belly, still stroking him but not getting any closer to where his member now stood stiffly away from his body. "You've made me get past my shyness. Your turn."

"Well . . . you climbed all over my body and then spread your legs and brought your pussy to my face," he said.

She moaned into his ear. Mostly for his benefit, but the images he was creating in her mind would work for her too. When they left here, she'd call them up as she used her vibrator.

"I'm getting excited, Ethan," she whispered. "You're making me wet."

"Do tell."

"In a minute, I'm going to touch you. I can't wait much longer," she said.

"Neither can I."

"Do you use a lubricant when you masturbate?" she asked. "Should I get something?"

"If you want. I don't really need it."

"You sure?" She touched him finally, brushing her fingertips along his shaft to the head.

"Holy . . . oh man." He grunted. "Nope, I don't need anything."

"I think I want to. I want you slick in my hand."

"Sit on me for a while. That'll do the job," he said.

"Nope. I want to watch everything." She got up and headed into the kitchenette. Cooking oil would work, but it would make a serious mess on the couch. Her eye settled on the liquid hand soap. Perfect. After running the water to get it warm, she moistened her hand and squirted some of the soap into her palm. When she'd worked it into a lather, she turned off the water and went back to Ethan.

"Here you go, big guy." She took him fully into her hand, wrapping her fingers around him. "This the right temperature?"

He groaned. "You'd feel better, but yeah. Oh yeah."

Now, she could watch as her hand stroked him. Poor baby had become so hard he barely fit inside his own skin. She moved slowly, enjoying the sight of him growing darker in color as he became more excited. He'd rested his head back against the couch, his face relaxing into an expression of bliss.

"Are you thinking about me now?" she said. "Are you imagining my pussy against your face."

"You taste so good when you're excited."

"I'm excited now." No lie there. Touching him this way, taking control of his arousal was a bigger turn-on than she'd imagined. She'd be completely wet in another minute. Maybe that would finally give her the courage to ask for the ultimate secret—his hand on her ass. The spanking she'd wanted for years but had never gotten up the nerve to ask for. Yes, she'd ask today.

"Getting close?" she asked.

"Make it last," he answered. "Never thought a hand job could feel so fucking good."

"I love doing it. You're so big and hard." For a bit of a change, she tugged at the head of his cock, twisting gently.

"Oh shit." His breathing became labored and erratic, and his cock had turned a livid color. A droplet appeared at the tip, signaling his impending orgasm. It was fascinating to watch him and incredibly erotic. When he made love to her, that happened inside her body. What a miracle.

"I'm gonna come. Oh, baby, now."

"Let's see if I can do this right." She picked up the pace of her strokes, gripping him firmly as her fist pumped him from the base to the tip. He released another drop of pearly liquid, and she massaged that into his skin. After a moment, a rumble built in his chest and rose in pitch and volume. His hips jerked upward as a spray of semen shot from him. Others followed, flying everywhere, landing on her hand and his stomach. Such a powerful response. Pride swelled in her chest that she could do this for him, along with gratitude that he'd allowed her to see.

After a few more seconds, his body went limp against the cushions. His eyes remained closed, his lips parted as he struggled for breath. Sighing, she released him and rested her own head near his.

"Thank you," she said.

"No, I thank you," he said. "Wow."

"You're an entertaining boy toy."

He groaned and chuckled. "Keep using me until you use me up."

"Is that possible?"

"Nuh-huh, but keep trying."

The time had come for her to ask him what she really wanted. Still satisfied from his orgasm, he might not even pay attention. Later, when the meaning sank in, he'd have had some time to let the meaning grow on him. Besides, it wouldn't seem so strange after what they'd just done. Women didn't masturbate men in the normal course of vanilla sex. A woman requesting a spanking was only a small step further into kink, right?

His eyes opened. "You got quiet all of a sudden."

She bit her lip. "I was just thinking."

"I like the look on your face," he said. "Share."

"Well, it seems to me that what we just did was pretty naughty."

"And . . ."

"I think maybe I ought to be spanked." She held her breath waiting for his reaction. Would the idea repulse him, excite him? Would he do it or push her away?

His brow furrowed. "You want me to hit you?"

"On my bottom, yes. I think you ought to use your hand to paddle me until I'm pink and warm."

He sat up straight. "I can't hit you. Only violent creeps hit women."

"Even if the woman asks for it?"

"I don't know." He blew out a breath. "I guess people play that way. I've never thought about doing it."

Well, that took care of that. She shouldn't have asked. She should have known that, if Ethan Gould had plenty of faults, violence wasn't one of them. Spanking probably really belonged only in her fantasies, anyway. Some things felt good to think about but wouldn't work in reality. Still, if he had limits on what he'd do, he should have told her from the beginning. Thank heaven she'd never see him again after they left this cabin, or the whole thing would be truly humiliating.

"It was just an idea," she said. "I think I'll get some work done."

"You're embarrassed, aren't you?"

Oh great, now they'd have a talk. "It doesn't matter. Really. You'd better power down your laptop before the battery dies."

"Shit. I really blew it. I told you anything goes, and the minute you get really creative, I turn all Puritan on you."

"My idea of kink is different from yours. It's not a big deal." She rose from the couch, but he grabbed her hand and pulled her back down.

"I'm getting pretty sick of this crap."

She pulled her hand back. "What in hell 'crap' are you talking about?"

"I told you no inhibitions, and you're pulling away from me."

Her jaw dropped as she stared at the idiotic man. "I told you what I wanted. It turned you off. We don't do it. That's all."

"When are you going to start standing up for yourself?"

"You're a real asshole, you know that?"

"You'd better watch who you're calling an asshole, young lady," he said.

What the . . . ? This didn't make any sense at all. He might be self-confident enough to be called cocky or ego-tistical, but she would never have thought him aggressive or nasty. Words fled, and she could only gape at him.

"I might have to put you in your place," he said. "I might have to teach you a lesson."

Wait a minute. Could he be playing along? "What kind of lesson?"

"The kind you won't be forgetting any time soon. The kind that'll make your fanny sore."

"You wouldn't really do that, would you?" He would, though, because she'd asked him to. He really would do whatever she wanted. Oh my God. Her dirtiest fantasy. She could have it. If it didn't work out, he'd stop, but if it did arouse her the way imagining it always had, what an experience it could give her.

"I don't want to spank you, but you've given me no choice," he said. "I only need to decide if you should be naked or not."

"Not naked, please." Of course, she was asking for the exact opposite. His hand on her bare flesh would hurt oh so good. Besides, the swats would make her pussy throb. Once he had her really excited, she'd need his hand everywhere—inside and out. "I'd be too embarrassed for you to see me undressed."

"Too bad. Get up and strip out of your clothes."

"If you say so," she said. "All right."

"I do . . . say so."

After removing her shoes and socks, she rose. She'd give him a striptease as she removed her clothing. After she removed her sweater, she toyed with the front closing of her bra, opening each clasp at a time. Once it was open, she shimmied out of it and cupped her breasts. "I touch these sometimes. It's naughty, but I like to tease the nipples until they're stiff."

She did that now. She'd not only meant the display for his entertainment but it also created a thrum of desire that went all the way to her sex. She had become aroused watching him come, and now, she'd get her own satisfaction. He might not be able to get hard again so soon, but he could use his hand or even his mouth to give her an orgasm.

Now, she went to her slacks, unfastening the waist band and then pulling the zipper down. Slipping her hand inside between her legs, she touched herself. When she brushed her clit, it responded with a sharp stab of desire. She gasped and followed that with a long "ahhh."

"What are you doing?" he said.

"Touching my pussy," she answered. "It feels so good."

"This is supposed to be punishment," he said. "Finish undressing and stretch out over my knees."

Obeying, she bent over a little and pushed her slacks and panties down and then stepped out of them. Now, she stood before him naked and aroused. She was so exposed, so vulnerable, and that risk excited her in a way that she'd never expected. Even better, his cock seemed to come to life again, swelling and growing longer.

"Hand me your panties," he ordered.

She scooped them up and handed them to him. Squeezing the material in his fist, he brought them to his nose. "Nasty, nasty girl. I'm going to make you sorry. Get over here."

How utterly bizarre and submissive and delicious.

She spread herself over his knees, her face pointed down toward the floor. She could have sworn something bumped against her side where something shouldn't be unless he had a hard-on. He was becoming aroused too, and given that he'd climaxed only moments ago, that meant he was finding this every bit as erotic as she was.

"Are you sorry for what you've done?" he said.

"You liked it," she answered.

"Shameless." The flat of his hand came down on one of her buttocks. His long fingers covered the whole expanse of flesh. "Do I have to hit you again?"

"You like that too."

"I see I have my work cut out for me." He hit her again, this time on the other buttock and rather harder than the first time.

He wasn't hurting her. He wouldn't do that. But if he could make her skin sting and feel warm, he'd have her squirming. This felt better than it had in her fantasies.

"Ready to apologize?" he said.

"Make me."

He slapped her a few more times. Thwap, thwap, thwap. Her sex throbbed, so close to where his hand came down on her. If he moved just a few inches, he'd touch the swollen lips of her pussy, and how good that would feel.

"I hate doing this to you, but it's for your own good." He hit her and hit her and hit her. Firmly but not violently. Bless him, he was getting the hang of it.

She couldn't hold still as the arousal built inside her. Arching her back, she offered the lips of her sex for his stroking. "Don't hit me anymore. I'll be good. I promise."

"You're lying. You just want me to play with your pussy, you sinful woman."

"No, truly. I'd die if you touched me. Anything, just don't touch me there."

"You're trying to tempt me." He slapped the backs of her thighs. Now, the warmth spread all around her most sensitive places. That made the throbbing only worse, and she released moisture into the hairs that covered her sex.

"Look at this," he said. "Wet."

"Don't touch it!"

Of course, he did exactly that, and she almost crawled out of her skin. She let loose a cry of excitement. *More, please more.*

"Disgraceful." He dipped a finger inside her. Her muscles clamped down around it. This was torture. Would he make her come soon? Would he keep her here, so close to the edge and not push her over? How long could he draw it out?

And had he become erect again? She twisted so that she could feel for his cock. Her fingers found it. Yes, hard. Miraculously, gloriously hard.

"Don't you ever learn?" he said, and he hit her again—really hard this time. She let out a yip of surprise as she almost lost herself and came.

"How would you like it if I did this?" He slipped his finger into her again and this time rubbed it over her hypersensitive clit.

Oh my God, oh my God . . . oh my God! He was taking her apart. Even in her wildest dreams, she'd never felt like this.

He kept doing it, dipping into her and then coating her most sensitive flesh with the moisture. She gasped and tensed as the orgasm approached. If he did that one more time . . .

"Now," she cried. "Oh now. Ethan. Please, please!"

In a moment, she found herself on her back on the couch, one foot dangling over the edge to spread her thighs. He loomed over her as he found his place and drove himself inside her. He'd filled her again. As he thrust, he hit her sweet spot over and over. She wrapped her legs around him as the whole world went crazy. Her body trembling, she gave in to the overwhelming rush of sensation. Deep inside it built and built until she could finally take no more and she climaxed, clutching at his hardness over and over.

She couldn't even scream but just hung onto him as he pounded into her a few more times roared with his own orgasm. He'd come again, the impossible, precious man.

When it ended, they collapsed together, both breathing hard. Reality returned, bringing with it total pleasure, total relaxation, total joy. She'd asked him for the ultimate, and he'd made it even better than she could have dreamed.

"Oh, baby." He covered her face with tiny kisses. "Damn, Laura. Promise me you'll never do this with anyone but me."

Her brain barely registered the words, let alone the meaning. He was right, in any case. She'd leave all the fantasy behind in this cabin. That was their deal. Only their deal had given her the freedom. He'd given her a gift she'd keep in her heart forever.

LAURA GLANCED UP from the eggs she'd been mixing for their breakfast and found Ethan leaning against the counter in that faux casual way he had when he planned to trot out the Gould charm to get something he wanted. Amazing, but he could pull it off wearing nothing but a robe and before he'd had his first cup of coffee.

"I didn't know you were awake," she said.

"I thought I'd sneak up and watch you acting domestic."

"Look closely. I don't do housewife," she said. "But even I have to eat."

"I'll cook, if you want."

"You've done enough." Oh brother, had he. She might have to find some kryptonite to slow him down. Her pussy had a pleasantly used ache that would remind her if her mind could manage to forget.

"There's coffee," she said.

"Great." He got a mug out of the cupboard, poured himself a cup, and then went back to lounging against the counter. "This has been really wonderful, Laura."

The direct address. She'd been in business long enough to know that when someone used your first name in a one-on-one conversation , when there could be no doubt of the target of the speech, it generally meant to convey intimacy. Heaven knew they'd been intimate, but mostly in a physical way.

"I'm glad your rental car couldn't make it through the snow," he said. "How about you?"

A definite manipulation. She could either agree with him or make herself appear like an insensitive lout. "It has been wonderful."

"I've been thinking . . ."

The toaster popped up at just that moment, stopping him mid-sentence.

"Excuse me." She walked around him and made a big show of buttering the toast before putting two more slices of bread in and pushing down the lever. Then, she had to get to the other side of him again to put the toast onto a plate and into the oven next to the bacon.

"As I was saying," he began.

"Would you get the juice out and put it on the table?"

He studied her for a second, clear displeasure showing in his gaze. "Sure."

While he carried out that task, she put some butter into the frying pan. When it melted, she added the chopped onion and waited for it to sizzle.

"Anything else you want me to do?" This time he stood closer to her, making it harder for her to avoid looking at him. She managed, though, stirring the onions around as if they required constant attention.

"I grated some cheese," she said. "I found only cheddar. I hope that's okay."

"Of course, it is."

"If we'd had bell pepper, Monterey jack would have been better, but I don't suppose that matters."

"I can honestly say that, in the cosmic scheme of things, cheese is not important right now."

"Good. I like cheddar too."

"Laura." He caught her wrist and turned her toward him.

"That's going to burn."

"Let it," he said. "We have to talk."

"Oh no, we don't."

He had the nerve to look surprised. "What?"

"You see, that's the way spouses speak to each other when they're upset," she said. "The last time I checked, you weren't my husband."

"We've been acting like husband and wife."

"We've been sleeping together."

He leaned toward her, almost closely enough for their noses to touch. "You call what we do sleeping?"

"Actually, no. You taught me another word," she said. "It starts with an *f*."

"We have not been fucking."

"Yes, we have, Ethan. Morning, noon, and night. It's been glorious." She pulled her hand from his, grabbed the bowl with the eggs, and tossed the mixture into the pan with the onion.

"Do you want to know what I think?" he said.

The other great ploy—on the surface, offering to share but in reality putting the opponent into the position of having to ask what the other person wanted. "Maybe later. I'm cooking our breakfast."

"Well, don't."

"What is wrong with you this morning? Just when I thought we were getting along so well." A manipulation of her own—establishing their former relationship as normal and desirable. He'd no doubt see through it, but the maneuver might buy her some time. Only, time for what? She couldn't avoid his "talk" forever. Sooner or later he'd think up another tack and then another. She could seduce him into more sex, but even he couldn't manage that 24-7.

"We are getting along," he said. "Or we were until a few minutes ago."

"Ethan." She could use the direct address on him too. "I don't know why you suddenly feel the need to make things complicated."

"Not complicated at all."

"Then, why do we need to talk?"

"Because I'm not letting you go when we leave here."

There, he'd said it. He'd been building up to this for a while. Calling her "baby" of all things. He'd even made that remark about her not doing "this" with anyone else. At the time, she'd tried to rationalize that away. Now she had to face it. For some reason, he'd taken it into his head to think of this arrangement as more serious than it was.

"I want more, Laura. I want to see what the future holds for us." He stood there, staring at her with a deadly serious gleam in his eyes. Fixing for a fight. She'd give him one.

"We had a deal," she said.

"I'm calling it off."

"You can't do that."

"Watch me," he said.

"Oh no." She held up her hands as if to ward him off. "You will not do this. You cannot do this."

"Why in hell not?"

"Because, the only way I could be this free with you was precisely because I wouldn't have to face what I'd done later on."

"Face?" he repeated, his voice rising. "What should you have to face? You haven't done anything wrong."

"I jerked you off, Ethan. I asked you to spank me."

"Last I heard, those things are legal between consenting adults."

"I don't do them," she said. "I'm a professional person with a reputation to protect."

"No one's going to know."

"You will," she said.

"So what?"

"I'll have to look at you, and I'll know that you know."

"That doesn't make any damned sense, Laura." He shoved his fingers through his hair, making it stick out in several directions. Nothing ever ruffled this man. Even matrix algebra hadn't had any effect on him that anyone could notice. She'd managed to rattle him. Quite an accomplishment. Too bad she couldn't enjoy the fact.

Something started to smell. Acrid, like something burning. She glanced at the stove. "The eggs. They're charcoal."

She reached for the pan, but he got it first and moved it to a cold burner. "I don't give a damn."

"I may have ruined that pan."

"I'll get Jeff another one."

"For heaven's sake." She reached under the counter for another frying pan. She'd started breakfast, so she'd finish it. They'd choke it down, and then she'd figure out some way to get away from him. Maybe she'd lock herself in the bathroom with her laptop and get some work done.

When she straightened and put the new pan onto the stove, he took that from her too. "I don't want any damned eggs. I want an explanation. Why can't we be together?"

"I'm not a person who jerks men off. I'm not a person who licks maple syrup off men's penises. I'm not a person who wants to be spanked," she said. "I could do those things only in this place for these few days. I have to leave them here."

He remained silent, gritting his teeth and leaning his fists against the counter.

Damn it all. He probably couldn't understand. He did what he wanted without guilt or second guessing himself. She'd never had that kind of freedom because her conscience would torment her with constant reminders of her improper behavior.

"Besides, there's something you seem to have forgotten," she said. "You and I are competing for the same job."

That seemed to startle him. He straightened. "I haven't thought about that since we got here."

And that startled her. They'd attended a top-tier business school and had both had rapidly rising careers. No matter what you thought of a person like Ethan Gould, you couldn't miss the success of one of your former colleagues. In the few days they'd been here, he'd actually forgotten about why they'd both ended up on the frozen highway to begin with.

Of course, her interview hadn't figured uppermost in her mind while he'd been showing her body such expert treatment. Maybe neither of them had concentrated on it a lot. What did that say?

"Neither of us are going to backstab the other," he said.

"Of course not."

"There's no reason we'd have to come out of the hiring process enemies, right?" he said. "Fair competition wouldn't hurt a personal relationship."

"The competition wouldn't, but one of us will end up settling here."

He stood there, his expression blank. He obviously hadn't put two and two together.

"And the other one won't," she said.

His face fell. "I see your point."

"Henderson is the only big outfit around here. One of us will have to go back to our current job or at least find something in another part of the country."

"That's a problem."

"A pretty big one, I think," she said.

He rubbed a hand over his jaw. "What say . . . well . . . if I were to get the job at Henderson—"

"Oh no." She held up a hand as if warding off a curse. "Don't even say it."

"Couples work this kind of problem out all the time."

Good Lord, the son of a bitch was really going there. He was going to suggest she give up her job so they could set up housekeeping. "The next words out of your mouth had better be to change the subject, Ethan Gould."

"Would it be so horrible?"

"I am not giving up my career to play house with you." Damn it. If she didn't pace for a while, she'd have to kill him. So she paced. "I can't believe you'd ask. I can't believe you'd even imagine it."

"Calm down. I was just thinking outside of the box."

"I'll put you in that box and six feet under if you ever . . . ever! . . . suggest such a thing again."

"It's just because I care about you, okay?"

He did appear upset, and he normally faked nonchalance. That didn't change the fact that, when push came to shove, he assumed she'd make the sacrifice of her career and not the other way around.

"We're both creative," he said. "We'll think of a way."

"After this, I don't think I trust your ways."

"Laura, see reason."

"No, you see reason. I thought a lot of things about you, but I never suspected you're the kind of man who'd make assumptions about a woman 'assuming the role.' "

He threw his hands in the air again. "What in hell does that mean?"

"That I'd act like the ladies auxiliary society. Play on the fringes. Act as your support system so that you could pursue a career while I look on from the sidelines."

"I didn't ask any such thing," he said. "I just want us to be together. Is that such a crime?"

"But it never occurred to you to give up your job to be with me."

"Of course, it did," he said. "Or it would have. I would have thought of that."

She crossed her arms over her chest and stared at him. Stupid man. They'd had world-class sex with each other for days. That was all this time together was supposed to be, and he had to go and spoil it.

A knock came at the door. Followed by a male voice. "Halloo, anyone home?"

"Go away," Ethan yelled back.

"You want your driveway plowed?" the voice called.

Plow. The obvious finally penetrated. The plows had come through. They could leave. She'd been so wrapped up in Ethan's stupidity she hadn't realized what the knock had meant.

"Yes, we want the driveway plowed," she called back as she headed to the doorway. When she opened it, she found a small man standing on the stoop. He was so bundled up, she could make out only blue eyes above a scarf. Behind him stood a huge pickup truck with a plow attached to the front. Farther away, the road had been cleared, probably during the night while they'd slept.

"I saw your truck in the carport and figured someone was here," the man said.

"We are. We'd very much appreciate you clearing the driveway so that we can leave."

Chapter Six

ETHAN WENT BACK into the cabin after stashing his bag in the back of the cab of his pick-up. Laura pointedly didn't look at him as she finished drying their dishes and putting the pans away. She'd pretty much avoided interaction after that ridiculous argument they'd had. Now, she expected to leave without working out how they could have a relationship. Clearly, she didn't feel the same way about him as he did about her. Didn't that just figure? He'd found a woman he wanted more from, and she had no interest in him.

She finally couldn't pretend he didn't exist any longer, but she still didn't look him in the eye when she turned. "Do you think there's enough hot water for me to take a shower now?"

"Should be."

She pointed toward the plastic bag that held their garbage. "We'll need to take this with us."

"I'll put it in the truck," he said. "You go ahead."

She did glance at him, briefly, before averting her gaze. He might have caught a tiny glimmer or regret or even guilt. She sure as hell didn't spit in his face as she'd done earlier. She wasn't all that happy to be kissing him off, it seemed.

Finally, she went into the bathroom and closed the door behind her. He got the garbage and headed toward the front of the cabin. When he got there, he stood with his feet rooted to the spot. Behind him, Laura would be shucking out of her robe. Getting naked. For the last time before their honeymoon-that-wasn't ended. Only an idiot would fail to take advantage of that situation.

He set the plastic bag down and turned. As he made his way to the bathroom, he stripped out of his jacket and shirt. A few steps farther, he unbuckled his belt and unzipped his fly. Before he could get rid of his jeans and shorts, he had to bend a little to take off his boots and socks, but he'd removed every stitch of clothing by the time he went into the bathroom.

The shower had already filled the tiny room with steam, but he could still make out the image of her figure behind the glass door. She hadn't noticed him, though, so he took a moment just to look at her, memorizing her every curve and movement. His cock did its thing, of course. He went from semiflaccid to fully erect in only seconds. It almost seemed to know that this would be its last treat for a while. After Laura, it would take him a long time to find another woman who interested him.

Damn her, anyway. How could she be so blind not to see that they had something irreplaceable?

Now ready for anything, even her resistance, he opened the shower door and climbed in with her. She jumped and gasped, and her hand went to her chest.

"It's only me," he said.

"Sorry. You just surprised me."

"I wouldn't let the guy with the plow in here to molest you," he said.

"I said I was sorry."

"Maybe I'm just being touchy."

She stared down at his hard-on, gazing at it almost wistfully, as if she missed it already.

"We don't have to leave this minute," he said. "Our deal isn't over yet."

"Was the deal until we left or until the plows showed up?"

"For the love of God, Laura, does it matter?"

She smiled at him. Finally, a sign that she hadn't erased him from her heart yet. The expression shouldn't have warmed his insides, but it did.

"Let me wash you," he said. "Then, you decide where we go from there."

She handed him the washcloth. "Do your damned-est."

He tossed the cloth to the floor. "I'll use my hands."

Extending her arms, she offered herself to whatever he wanted to do, and that particular subject covered a lot. First, he took her in his arms and kissed her. She'd already lathered herself, so her body felt slick against his. She fit against him perfectly, his cock snuggled against her belly.

After a few moments of sampling her lips, he could scarcely get the moist air into his lungs. She was breathing hard too, when he released her mouth and held her head against him. They stood that way for a bit, not saying anything, while her heart beat against his.

"I'm going to miss this," he said finally.

"Ethan, don't start."

"Okay, I'm done trying to convince you. I'm going to show you what you'll be missing."

She didn't push him away. She didn't even stiffen. She just stood there, not fighting but not encouraging him either. All the permission he needed.

Dipping his head, he placed his mouth against her ear and circled his tongue around the edge. Of course, his breath slipped inside, and she let out a tiny moan.

"I want you to remember that. And this." He sampled the length of her throat, running his lips and tongue downward and even nipping here and there. That got him a sigh. So far, so good. Pulling her against him, he pressed his erection into her belly. He didn't even have to ask her to remember that. Let her try to forget.

In fact, she tried to reach between them to touch him, but he stopped her hand. "Not yet. I'm not through giving you memories to take away."

"I want it."

"Coward. You mean you want me."

She hesitated. "I want you."

"You'll have me. No worries there."

Now, he bent lower and licked the underside of her breast. A trace of soap remained, but it made her all the more delicious. The spray of the shower pounded in droplets over his face as he moved to the nipple and took it into his mouth. He sucked until it hardened into a pebble. With her fingers in his hair, she swayed backward.

"Remember that too." He moved to the other breast and loved that too, until the sound of her breathing bounced off the walls to fill the small enclosure. So responsive, so passionate. She might use iron willpower to walk away from him, but she'd suffer from missing him. He'd miss her like hell too, but at least, he'd have the satisfaction of knowing that he'd tried to go with her into the future.

Now on to the ultimate. Kissing every inch of her flesh that he could reach, he sank to his knees in front of her. When he eased her legs apart, she touched his face.

"I can't," she whispered.

"You want me to stop?" He hadn't meant to make that sound hurt. But it would hurt if she denied him the ultimate taste of her before he had to say good-bye. He wouldn't back off, though. He stayed right where he was with water running down his face and landing on his shoulders.

"No, go on," she said as she moved her hand to the back of his head to urge him forward.

Thank heaven. She moved her feet, opening herself for his kiss. Taking what she offered with the reverence it deserved, he placed his mouth over her sex and stroked the lips with his tongue. Already, she'd become aroused enough to release her honey onto his face. Sweet and herbal, it tasted of her the way he'd remember her—excited and wanting him.

Now, he parted the petals and licked the inside, searching for her clit. It wasn't hard to find as it had stiffened into a tight bud. When he stroked it with his tongue, she trembled and gasped. Somehow, she continued to act surprised when she should have realized what he could do for her. But then, making love with this woman felt different every time.

She always had some new gift for him, and that made him feel like the greatest lover in the world. Good. Let her remember that too, when she lay alone in her bed and thought about him. She would. She might talk a good game about not needing him, but they both knew better.

He continued caressing her most sensitive flesh, using different rhythms and pressures, until she wobbled. Catching her hips in his hands to support her, he kept right on driving her wild until the rising inflection of her moans told him her orgasm was near. He could make her come this way, but he could also bring her to completion with his member embedded inside her. And that's what he'd have to torture himself with in the months and years ahead.

He released her hips and rose. "Grab onto the shower head."

For a moment, she didn't seem to understand his words, and no wonder. He'd brought her so close to the edge. When his meaning registered, she turned and reached upward to grip the faucet. Parting her legs, she offered her ass for his admiration. He could have gone down on his knees again to cover it with kisses, but she needed him inside her, and honestly, he'd go crazy himself in another few minutes.

He had to spread her thighs farther apart and squat to get the head of his member between her lips, but when he did, the reward more than paid off the effort. She seemed tighter than usual, clasping him firmly as he straightened and buried himself in her pussy. Tilting her head back, she let out a long "ahhh." The sort of sound that told a whole story in one syllable. Lust that could turn to love, if she'd let it. If only she'd admit the truth to herself.

He couldn't straighten completely without lifting her feet off the floor, but he could stay in this position for as long as he had to, to satisfy them both. Honestly, it wouldn't take long to finish her, and her orgasm would trigger his own, as it always did. He thrust slowly for a while, letting her feel the passage of his flesh inside hers. He wouldn't rush their last encounter but would savor it.

"I want you to remember this too," he whispered into her ear as he moved and moved.

"I won't forget," she whispered back. Something of an admission. He'd take it.

"I want you so much, Laura." He couldn't use the *l* word. It would only scare her. "I want to feel you like this always."

This time, she didn't answer, unless you counted her little cries. Poor baby. He'd made her really hot, and now he wanted promises. Instead, he kept giving her what her body craved. All of him from the base of his cock to the head. His body wouldn't let him go slowly now. It demanded release. Soon he'd have no choice but to come. Damn, but life sucked sometimes. In a perfect world, he could keep at this for hours. No, in a perfect world, he'd never have to let this woman out of reaching distance.

She shuddered and let out a little cry of need. Enough. He couldn't deny her—or himself—any longer. After reaching an arm around her, he buried his fingers into her pussy hairs and found her distended clit. When he touched it, she nearly floated off the floor, and her shout filled the tiny space. He rolled it between his thumb and forefinger, and she snapped. Crying out, she gripped him as her orgasm claimed her. Powerful contractions along the length of his cock. As he'd known would happen, his body burst into orgasm as the tension built and then broke free. He gritted his teeth as his lust spilled from him in waves.

Eventually, it ended, of course, and he returned to reality—more or less. He was still inside her, after all. But the sound and feel of spraying water returned, and his heart started to slow down to something approaching normal. His legs trembled from being crouched for so long, so he removed himself from her body and turned her so that she rested against his chest.

Neither of them spoke. What would they say? He'd laid out his feelings. He'd made a bad mistake at even hinting that she quit her job to stay with him, but she couldn't hate him for wanting her. She'd come to want him too. No way could she have shared herself with him as she had without some emotion. As stubborn and self-controlled as she was, though, she'd force herself to get over him. Shit.

He held her until the water turned cold. When she pushed away from him to turn it off, he left the shower without saying another word.

LAURA STARED AT the cursor on the screen of her laptop. She shouldn't have to sweat so much over this e-mail. Executives moved around all the time. Her boss, Joe Sampson, would make all the usual noises—offer more money, tell her how valuable she was to the company—and then, he'd go find someone perfectly capable of filling her position. Why wouldn't the words come?

Hell, she didn't have a problem with this e-mail. She had a problem with everything since she'd left a certain cabin up in the mountains. She and Ethan had scarcely spoken ten words after he'd left the shower, but his expression had spoken for him. Loud and clear. She'd hurt him. He wasn't faking it, wasn't manipulating her to get his way. He really did have feelings for her, and she'd pushed him away.

Ethan Gould, drop-dead handsome charmer-of-women and glad-hander-of-all. Most likely to succeed while making it look easy. Mr. Popularity. That man had fallen for her. How could she have anticipated *that* happening? She couldn't, of course, and she'd had no way of handling it when it did happen. With her quiet nature and relative inexperience with men, how could she comprehend such a thing happening?

What if? What if she'd given the possibility some thought? Might they have worked something out? Might she be in his arms right now?

More important, what if she'd been wrong? Could she really leave the forbidden parts of herself behind? She'd still have all those longings, perhaps even stronger now that she'd experienced her hidden desires and recognized their power. She'd had a man she could trust to keep what happened between them private. The same man who'd do anything she wanted and put his whole heart into it. How could she have rejected a man like that?

"I'm an idiot," she said to the computer screen. "A stupid, fucking idiot."

He'd had one thing right. She'd remember everything, not just from their last encounter in the shower but from the moment when he'd climbed into the loft and rolled his body onto hers. She'd remember his touch, his scent, the taste of his mouth. She'd remember his smile, his laughter, even his cooking. Any lover she might allow in her bed would fall short in so many categories.

She powered down the laptop and closed it. Resting her fist on the desk, she closed her eyes and tipped her head back. She'd have a mammoth headache if she kept thinking of this. She'd get on with her life. She had all the craziness of a new job and a move across country. She wouldn't have time to moon over a man.

A knock came on the door, followed by a muffled male voice with a heavy accent she couldn't place. "Room service."

"I didn't order anything," she called back.

"Room service," he said again.

Men. Did they all have it in for her lately? She got up and went to the door. "I didn't order anything."

This time, his answer was garbled enough that she couldn't make it out at all. She opened the door.

A man stood on the other side, hidden behind a bouquet of helium balloons. In his free hand, he held a wine bucket with the neck of a champagne bottle sticking out the top.

"I didn't order anything," she said for the third time. He ignored her and brushed past her into the room.

Well, this was a nice distraction. She could chew on him for a few minutes and forget her troubles. That ought to get rid of her headache.

When he released the balloons and they floated up to the ceiling, she almost smacked herself for being so obtuse. "Ethan."

He set the wine bucket on the table and pulled the bottle out. "I hear congratulations are in order."

"Yeah. I'm sorry I beat you for the job."

"Don't be," he said. "I'm glad for you."

Which brought them to the question of why he'd come here. He might have only meant to give her good wishes, but the look on his face—a combination of slyness and happiness to see her—said he had more reasons for this visit. Sex, no doubt. One last one-night stand.

She crossed her arms over her chest. "You're glad you lost the job opportunity."

"Yup. You know the expression that when the universe closes a door, a window opens or something like that?"

"You're going into the platitude business?"

He pulled the cork from the champagne. It made a loud pop but didn't gush wine, thank heaven. "Glasses?"

"Ethan, what are you doing?"

"Never mind. I'll find them myself." He disappeared inside the bathroom. After a moment, he reappeared with two plastic glasses, each half full. He held one out to her and didn't move until she took it.

"Here's to your new job." He lifted his glass in a toast. "And here's to our new negotiations."

She paused in the act of sipping her champagne and lowered her glass. "What new negotiations would those be?"

"For our continuing partnership. You see, I'm calling bullshit on all your reasons we have to say good-bye."

"Oh really."

"You see, for a brilliant mind, you came up with some amazingly dumb premises," he said. "First, that you're not the sort of person who likes sucking on cocksicles or watching your lover come or getting your little butt slapped. You do like those things."

She didn't answer. What could she say? She'd pretty much decided the same thing just before he came in.

"And you know what? There's nothing wrong with

that," he went on. "The only sin is trying to deny your own nature."

"Thank you, Dr. Freud. Be sure to send a bill."

"Joke all you want," he said. "You know I'm right."

"Okay." She took a gulp of her wine. "You are."

"I am?" His jaw dropped. "That is, damned straight I am."

"So, what are we negotiating now?" She looked him straight in the eye. She had a pretty good idea what his answer would be.

"A future, Laura. I'm not settling for anything else."

"We've been through this. We'll be in separate parts of the country. I'm not going to see my lover on alternate weekends." For heaven's sake, she'd actually used the word lover in relation to Ethan Gould.

"That was your second dumb premise," he said. "Do you honestly think I'd accept an arrangement like that?"

"So, where are you going to work? Beaumont's store?"

"I've wanted to start my own business for years, but I couldn't think of anything I had a real passion for," he said. "Now, I have. Mountain cabins."

"Like your friend's." The one where she'd spent the finest days of her life. With him.

"I did some research, worked up some spreadsheets and a business plan," he said. "Jeff and I are going into business. Right here."

"You'll make a mint."

"I plan to, which brings me to the last question." He took her glass and set both of their drinks on the desk.

Then he turned back to her and, without asking permission, put his arms around her and pulled her against his chest. "Where do you and I go from here?"

"Go?" she repeated. "I didn't know we had travel plans."

"Oh, we do." The light of mischief in his amber eyes warmed into something more lethal. Not the easy charm she'd seen dozens of times but the knowledge they shared of each other—a connection that would take months or years to break, if it could be broken at all.

"I'm going to take you to heaven and back. Multiple times a day," he said. "Now that I'm staying here, you can move in with me."

"I don't suppose I have any say in the matter."

"We can haggle for a while." He gave her a slow grin. "I'll win in the end."

She couldn't help but gaze up into his face. "Insane, obstinate man."

"I see I have to sweeten the deal," he said. "Okay. Besides my talents in the sack, I'm a pretty good cook."

"That you are."

"I won't stick you with all the housework. I'll even do your laundry."

"Now, I know you're crazy," she said. "A man doing laundry?"

"You bet. Where else are you going to find an offer like that?"

"Nowhere, I guess." Why should she continue to fight the inevitable? He'd solved the geography problem. She'd see him around town, if not by coincidence then because he'd put himself in her way. When she saw him, she'd want him. She'd end up spending all her free time in his bed. They might as well combine households so that he'd be around all the time to scratch her sexual itches. "All right, you've convinced me."

He heaved a sigh of relief. "Finally."

"You were worried? Ethan Gould thought a woman could refuse him?"

"The stakes were high. I didn't have anything better to offer than laundry."

"Oh, but you know you did." She wiggled against him, creating friction against the front of his pants.

He made a soft growling noise in his throat. "Good thing we're near a bed."

"Ah, but negotiations aren't over yet," she said. "I have one more demand."

"Anything."

"Build me one of those cabins."

"You got it, baby."

This time, he kissed her for real. His mouth captured hers with his usual skill, teasing and cajoling until she could scarcely breathe for all the joy of having him again. Her heart sped up, and her blood pounded in her ears. She could have him now. Over and over. Whenever and however she wanted him. Soon, the whole universe disappeared except for the lips on hers, the arms that held her, and his firm body against her softer one.

After a minute, he pulled back, his breath coming hard. "Is it hot in here?"

"Definitely."

"Heat rises."

She eased her hand between their bodies, searching for the impression of his swelling member and finding it. "It certainly does."

Keep reading for an excerpt from

STORM BOUND,

the next book in Alice Gaines's
steamy Cabin Fever series,
coming in July 2012
from Avon Red

Chapter One

CHRISTIE LOVEJOY STARED glumly at the image of the natural disaster that was going to ruin her sex life. Thanks to the resort's wifi, she could sit on the terrace in sun-drenched paradise and follow the approaching weather patterns on her laptop. A certain bastard named Fred was building to a fierce tropical storm. He'd soon become a hurricane and come crashing over Santa Inez Island. Her guests—the potential clients she'd lured here so they could send huge amounts of business to her company's latest project—would have to evacuate or be stuck here for several days.

The phrases "her sex life" and "potential clients" didn't belong anywhere near each other, of course. Very bad business practice. But her libido was getting ready to make an exception for these two. Instead of middle-aged-men with wedding rings and more paunch than hair, fate had sent her two fine male specimens. They'd arrived to spend three days with her in almost total isolation in one of the most romantic locations on Earth. Sunny days and balmy nights with no one else to distract them. That was until Fred had decided to crash the party.

Not far from her table, Wolf Martin and Jon Tucker were engaged in a game of one-on-one basketball. Most people, when offered miles of pristine beaches and warm breezes would stretch out under an umbrella and read a book or doze off. These two swam—hard—racing each other with firm strokes. When Wolf won that, Jon challenged him to hoops, which they entered with the same savage competitive spirit. You'd think them enemies instead of friends and partners. No matter. All this physical play gave her a view of their bodies in motion, and what a feast for the eyes that was.

Jon used his height advantage to soar over his partner as he approached the net for a dunk. Muscles in his back and shoulders flexed. Not an ounce of extra flesh or unnecessary movement marred his perfection as he arced through the air. Wolf didn't back down but charged up under him, tangling his arms with Jon's to block the shot. The two seemed to hang in the air, frozen in time. A work of erotic art Michelangelo could have created if he had sculpted with human flesh.

How in hell was she supposed to keep her mind on business with that going on just out of her reach? Watching the two of them in action would send any healthy female's imagination into overdrive. Hers had certainly slipped into high gear as she imagined each of them as her lover.

Jon would feel smooth under her palms as she eased her hands down his back to his buttocks, feeling the muscles work as they coupled. He'd go slowly at first. Exploring. And then faster as they became more and more aroused until they came, clutching at each other.

Or she'd have Wolf. All animal, that one, right down to his name. He'd appeared almost tame in his business suit. Now he looked as if he could burst out of his swim trunks and snug t-shirt. Where Jon floated gracefully, Wolf charged. He'd be the same in the sack. No nonsense. Just the sort of fast, hard fuck that could overpower his lover with orgasm after orgasm.

Damn it all. She shouldn't become this excited just watching two men playing basketball, no matter how attractive. She especially shouldn't put herself into a position where she could embarrass herself over potential business partners. She should be pointing out the assets of the resort and how it made a perfect location for their trademark adventure and sensuality tours. Yet, here she sat with her heart racing and her pussy muscles clenching in hopes of finding hard male flesh to fill her. Maybe tropical storm Fred would do her a favor, after all, and get the two of them away from her before she disgraced herself completely.

"No points for that. You fouled me," Wolf said. The streaks of gray at his temples gave him a salt-and-pepper coloring, much like the fur of a silver wolf. With angular features and piercing blue eyes, he had an air of danger to him. Definitely predatory but in a way that made the prey want to be captured.

"Bullshit," Jon answered. "You're playing out of your league."

Jon stood a few inches taller than Wolf and used his height to his advantage. He went right up to his partner, staring down at him. His long fingers allowed him to hold the ball in one hand. A caress of sorts, the way he might palm her breast.

"We'll ask Christie." Wolf turned toward her. "Did he foul me or not?"

"Hmm?" She mentally shook away the forbidden images in her head. "Sorry. I wasn't watching."

That wasn't exactly a lie. She hadn't taken her eyes off either of them since they'd stepped out of the hotel wearing their swim trunks. But as closely as she'd scrutinized their every movement, she hadn't paid any attention to the ball or followed the rules of the game. She'd been too busy fantasizing about finding herself trapped between them while four hands roamed over her, unclasping her bra and cupping her breasts, or strong fingers dipping into her panties to find her wet and ready.

"See?" Jon said. "She agrees with me."

"Grow up, will you?" Wolf loped over to her table, picked up a bottle of water, and took a long drink. This close, she could almost feel heat rolling off him. Probably just a breeze warmed by the sun, but it carried some kind of pheromone that sent a primitive signal to her brain. Male.

"I'm sorry my partner is behaving so unprofessionally," he said.

"Not a problem. We want you two to experience the resort the way your customers will," she said.

Wolf tugged his t-shirt over his head and used it to wipe away a sheen of sweat. One drop remained, trickling slowly down the center of his torso toward his trunks. It would probably taste like the salt from the edge of a margarita if she had the guts to lean over and lick it away. She didn't, though. Neither did she let her gaze drift downward into more dangerous territory. She'd tried that maneuver with both of them earlier and luckily hadn't been noticed. She couldn't stay lucky forever.

When she glanced back up, she met an assessing stare from Wolf. If he hadn't read her mind, his own thoughts were traveling in the same direction. Both of the men had been sending signals since they'd arrived the afternoon before. Much of their masculine display seemed calculated to win her favor, the way male animals vied for mates in the wild. She'd dated as much as the next woman and had taken her share of lovers over the years. But she'd never had two men in competition for her before.

The knowledge made her lightheaded. She only had to let them fight for her favors and decide which one to accept and under what terms. At least she would have—if the tropical storm had chosen some other place to make landfall.

"We've been enjoying ourselves," Wolf said. "That doesn't excuse my partner's foul language."

Jon stopped dribbling, tucked the ball under his arm, and yelled, "Sanctimonious prick."

"Asshole." Wolf turned and flung his t-shirt in the general direction of his partner.

Christie had to laugh. "I thought you two were friends."

"We are." Wolf pulled out a chair and sat across from her. "We close ranks in negotiations."

"I hope to experience that for myself soon."

One eyebrow went up. "The resort?"

"Of course."

"Because, um . . . He leaned closer, his blue gaze meeting hers. "There's something else the two of us can negotiate alone."

There it was. The opening volley. She'd give him an answer that indicated her interest, and they'd work out the details. Her heart fluttered in her chest. Until she remembered that damnable Fred.

Before she had a chance to respond, Jon joined them. Well over six feet tall and with sandy hair and bronzed skin, he might have been a sun god. Even the soft brown of his eyes appeared golden in the right light. Right now, those eyes were trained on her breasts, and when he finally looked into her face, he sent the same message silently that his partner had just put into words. He wanted her. Oh sweet Lord.

"So what's on for this evening?" Jon asked. It might have sounded innocent except for the light of sexual interest in his gaze.

"Nothing, I'm afraid." She turned the laptop toward them. "There's a hurricane on its way. We have to evacuate."

"Evacuate?" Wolf glanced up at Jon and then back to her. "I thought this resort was hurricane proof."

"We are, except for the most extreme. This won't cause much damage, if any." She'd already filled them in on the details of the resort. The hotel sat high enough on a hill above the ocean to escape even the highest storm surge. Most of their power came from solar cells that stored electricity created on sunny days. What appeared to be an exercise in pure luxury was actually more a triumph of engineering. They'd listened with interest to it all. Nothing could survive a major hurricane, but the Santa Inez Resort could weather a minor one with ease.

"If everything's going to be fine, why should we leave?" Jon asked. "Isn't that one of the appeals of Santa Inez—that a customer could witness a storm in the tropics without giving up the good life?"

"If they have the time to get stuck here. That's also a selling point—they can extend their vacation at our expense," she said.

"So, you're saying if we don't leave now we might have to stay longer than we'd planned," Wolf said.

"We'll be fine, but the surrounding area won't. Every available boat will join in search and rescue," she said. "The airport will probably shut down."

"How long?" Jon asked.

"There's no way of knowing." She shrugged. "Fred might fizzle out, or he might get stronger. Everything might get back to normal in a day or two, or it could take more like a week."

"I see." Jon ran his fingers through his hair. "I have contract negotiations in New York on Wednesday."

"And I'm meeting with Komura the day after that." Wolf sighed. "We need his business."

Well, there went the last hope. They *could* make a rationale for remaining here: if their company was to guarantee a tropical island trip during hurricane season, they'd need to know that the resort lived up to its billing for safe and comfortable accommodations. But they couldn't stay if it meant as much as a week away from their business.

These two executives probably never stayed in one place for more than a few days at a time. They couldn't afford to get stuck somewhere with no idea of when they could get out. Fred had, indeed, ruined her chances at every woman's hottest dream.

"When do we have to leave?" Wolf asked.

"The ferry will be here in about an hour," she answered. "My skeleton crew left on the morning run."

"That's that, then." Wolf placed his palms on the table top and rose. "I'll go pack."

"Me, too," Jon said, although he didn't move from the spot.

Wolf headed toward the main building. A few yards away, he stopped and turned back. "Are you coming?"

"Sure. Just a second," Jon called.

Wolf hesitated before resuming his path and disappearing inside.

Still Jon didn't walk away but stared at her a bit longer. "Too bad."

"I'm sorry you couldn't stay longer." Make that "we" couldn't stay longer. She'd have to evacuate, too.

"I'll see you in New York?"

"If my company wants me to negotiate the deal." She didn't normally serve in that capacity, though. In any case, things would be different in a big city with its distractions. They wouldn't have the same sexual charge in the air every minute of the day. Even if the two of them came back to the resort after it opened, they'd be surrounded by crowds and she'd have her hands full taking care of guests. Sometimes life gave, and sometimes it took away. This time sure sucked.

"Guess I'd better go, too," he said finally.

"I'll let you know when the ferry arrives."

WHEN THE TIME came, Christie had to use every ounce of will power to make her feet take her to the dock. As she descended the steps that led to the ocean, she passed the plantings the gardeners had so carefully arranged to look haphazard, wondering how roughly Fred would treat them. Most weren't native to the island but had been chosen for the ability to thrive in ocean breezes and sunlight filtered through the palms overhead. The tiny pink orchid flowers had just begun to open. Would they be here when she came back?

It was stupid, really, to worry about things here. The whole sales pitch about safety and security had facts to back it up. Still, she'd so much rather stay and see for herself. Tomorrow, she could check on things if she remained. More important, she could explore her sexual opportunities with Wolf and Jon if they remained with her.

When she arrived at the beach, she stepped onto the dock and walked to the end where the ferry would stop. Sighing, she set her few bags down and waited for her "rescue." The ferry wasn't far away, and now it puttered closer and closer. She really ought to go back up and collect her guests. Though the first clouds hadn't appeared yet, the storm was bearing down on them. They didn't have much time to get to the airport and get a flight out.

Captain Joe stood at the helm of the small vessel. When he got to the dock, he tossed her a line, which she tied around a piling. With no more than a dozen seats on benches, the boat hardly qualified as a ferry. No one occupied them now. He'd come for only Jon Tucker, Wolf Martin, and her.

Captain Joe smiled at her and then glanced behind her. "Where are the rest of the passengers?"

"At the hotel. Finishing packing." That wasn't true. They'd probably finished long ago. She just hadn't told them the ferry had arrived. Why did this have to be so damned hard?

"They'd best hurry. I have to get my boat back and stowed before the storm hits."

"Uh, yeah," she said.

"Christie? Is everything okay?"

Christie could not make herself answer. The memories crashed through her mind, tumbling over each other. Her first glimpse of the two businessmen, dressed in suits as if they had to impress her. They hadn't needed to dress formally to do that, but the elegant cut of their clothing had emphasized their lofty position on the corporate food chain. An easy exercise of power, a pure aphrodisiac. Then, they'd turned into beach bums, endearingly boyish.

Oh hell, all that was nice, but the sizzling glances sealed the deal. Jon's easy, knowing smiles. Wolf's suggestion they open personal negotiations. Every cell in her body knew by instinct that she could have one or both of them. Every primitive part of her brain promised to punish her for months, if not years, with fantasies of what could have been. Only the tiny part of her mind called "rational" or "conscience" told her to let them go. The "want" and "must have" parts could squash rationality and doing the right thing like a bug. In fact, they did.

Squish. Dead.

She might as well face facts. She wasn't letting Jon and Wolf off this island until she'd explored every inch of their bodies or died trying.

"Christie?" Captain Joe rubbed his chin in puzzlement. "Talk to me."

"Right." She smiled, returning his gaze as innocently as possible. "What I meant to say is, I'm sorry you came all the way out here for no reason."

"I always come out here at this time of day."

"Of course, but you must have preparations to make before the storm closes in."

He continued to study her as if she wasn't making any sense. Maybe she wasn't, but one way or another, she had to get him to turn his ferry around and leave before one of the men realized their escape from getting trapped here had arrived.

"There's still some time to get back to the mainland ahead of the storm," the captain said. "But I don't know when I'll get back out here."

"Good, you go on. The two executives have sent for their own boat," she said.

"They have a boat?"

"Their company does. You know how these business types are. They like their luxury."

"You're sure?" Captain Joe rubbed the back of his neck. "I didn't see anyone."

"Absolutely sure. It should be here in half an hour or so."

"What about you?" he asked.

"I'll go with them. We'll be fine. All three of us." That had all come out too high-pitched and too fast. She didn't lie often enough to be good at it.

"Okay then. I'll shove off." He didn't move for a moment, though, but kept studying her. She gave him what ought to look like an innocent smile—she didn't normally practice those, either—and met his gaze head on, even though her heart was pounding in her chest. If they stood here much longer, either Wolf or Jon was bound to appear. Not only would she have to say good-bye to them, but Captain Joe would no doubt ask them about their company's boat.

"You take care," Captain Joe said after what seemed

like ten minutes but could hardly have been more than a few seconds.

"Oh I will." She'd take care of herself by taking care of the two men—first one then the other. She bent to untie the line from around the piling and tossed it to Captain Joe so he could cast off. When he opened the throttle and directed the ferry away from the shore, she waved to him. Finally, he and his craft became no more than a speck on the horizon, and she turned to go up the path to the hotel, taking her first deep breath since he'd arrived. She left her bags to collect later and headed back to the hotel.

Neither her guests nor their luggage had made an appearance, so they wouldn't have seen the ferry arrive or leave unless they'd been watching from the terrace, and she'd seen no evidence of that. Now she only had to concoct some story for why the three of them had been stranded. An emergency on another island ought to work. Someone who'd had to be hurried to medical care. She'd think of something before she had to confront them.

Instead of worrying about that, she let the fantasies run free while she climbed the steps again, walking beneath the palm trees toward the huge windows overlooking the terrace and the sea. Reinforced shatter-proof glass, they should weather a gale bigger than Fred would create. They'd get quite a view of turbulence outside while they enjoyed themselves inside.

Wolf and Jon. Which one should she have first? The tall blond with the easy smile, or the smaller more intense man with the fierce blue gaze?

Oh sweet Lord. She stopped in her tracks for a moment. Or . . . she could have them both together. Two such competitive males. Could she get them to work together to give her sex more erotic than she'd ever hoped for? A threesome, her very own. She could have them both at once . . . a cock inside her while she sucked on another one. When one man tired, the other could take over. They could go on for hours that way.

But why stop there? Oh my. Once all inhibitions had dropped, they could experiment with anything that came to mind. They could role-play, say horny wife with the next door neighbor when her husband comes home unexpectedly. Or better—she could let them dominate her. She'd admired their easy sense of power from the first moment she'd set eyes on them. She could experience that directly. Total surrender to their sexual needs and her own. Just imagining it made her knees weak. Oh my God, could she really have that?

Not only could she have any sexual fantasy that occurred to them, but she could have them completely to herself with no one looking on and judging. No gossips. No stories to get out. She could indulge herself in every way possible. The only limits she'd have to face would be Jon and Wolf's reservations, if they had any.

She was risking a lot. A hell of a lot. Losing their business, for one thing, if they found out she'd lied. And if they were angry enough to tell the company why they'd bailed on Santa Inez, there went her job, too. Perhaps the worst would come if she had to face their anger and disappointment. That didn't make much sense, given that she'd met them only the day before. But she'd enjoyed Jon's easy smiles and Wolf's approval of everything she's shown him at the resort. Seeing all that evaporate because of her dishonesty would hurt. She could end up miserable and unemployed, all because she couldn't control her hormones.

She couldn't change that now. All she could do was hope for the best and enjoy herself. Perhaps if she did a really good job of making them happy, they'd forgive her if they did find out.

Damn it all, what was wrong with her? The only way they could learn of her deception was to talk to Captain Joe, and they had no way of doing that. She picked up her pace until she fairly skipped up the last few steps.

When she arrived inside the hotel, they were both waiting for her, luggage on the floor between them. Neither beach bums nor captains of industry now, they wore casual clothes—lightweight shirts and slacks. No matter how they dressed, they were mighty fine to look at. Now maybe she'd have the chance to feel Jon's long arms around her and burrow into the firm planes of Wolf's chest.

Jon bent to grab the handle of his suitcase. "Ferry waiting?"

"Uh no." *Think, think.* She needed a story when all her current thoughts came through x-rated. "There was an emergency on another island. High-risk pregnancy. She had to get to the mainland in case she needed a hospital in the next couple of days."

The two men exchanged glances.

"You mean the ferry left without us?" Jon asked.

"It never came," she answered. "I got a message on my cell phone."

"We're stranded?" Wolf asked.

"I'm afraid so," she said. "There's no time to get another boat out here in front of the storm."

"And none likely to come soon after the storm, either?" Wolf asked.

"I'm sorry."

Neither gave much of a clue as to how he felt about being stuck here. They couldn't be happy about missing their business engagements or they would have volunteered to stay. They didn't convey any skepticism about her story. But neither of them was dancing with joy.

"Look at it this way . . . I'll get to show you that the resort can weather even a mild hurricane," she said. "I think you'll be impressed."

"What about electricity?" Wolf asked.

"We have a generator and solar power," she said. "We were getting ready to open, so there's plenty of food and a well-stocked bar and wine cabinets."

"And a restaurant kitchen to play around in." Jon finally gave a clue to some emotion as the light of competitive mischief entered his eyes. "My partner here claims he knows how to use a chef's knife. What do you bet he's blowing smoke?"

Wolf heaved a sigh. "You never give it a rest, do you?"

Christie almost matched his sigh with one of her own, out of relief. If they were upset with her, they weren't showing it.

"We'll see who can really cook," Wolf said.

"That we will," Jon answered. That might be innocent enough except for the way they were both staring at her. With any luck, they'd all three be cooking by that evening.

"Do you buy her story?"

Jon pulled his head from the restaurant freezer long enough to glance at his friend and partner. Wolf stood on the other side of the butcher-block worktable, an open beer in his hand.

"Ms. Lovejoy's?" he said.

"She's the only 'her' around here," Wolf answered.

"What makes you think she lied?"

Wolf lifted one shoulder in a shrug. "It just seemed strange. One minute, we were all ready to go. The next, there was a mysterious cell phone message."

Jon thought back. He'd been too busy concentrating on how the top of her sundress stretched over her breasts to notice much of anything else. But she might have avoided their eye contact. Bad liars did that. Wolf had a great sense for people. He might be on to something.

"Do you really care if she's telling the truth?" Jon asked.

"Don't you?"

"I guess." Although he hadn't managed to push his fantasies of a naked Ms. Christie Lovejoy completely to the back of his mind, the state-of-the-art professional kitchen made for a pleasant diversion from the constant state of semi-arousal he'd endured since noticing how she moved—as if she were dancing with a man who really turned her on. Gleaming stainless steel appliances, more sauté pans than he could ever hope to dirty, and a six-burner gas stove with enough BTUs to fire up hell itself. All that could entertain him until he could watch her face when he first sank his cock into her.

"We're getting a free vacation in a gorgeous location," he said. "Don't over-analyze it."

Wolf took a drink of his beer while he considered that. "It's a matter of principle. Deception like that rubs me the wrong way."

Jon studied Wolf for a minute. "Why are you twisting yourself into knots about this? We won't even be dealing with her after we leave here."

"I like my lovers to be honest with me."

Jon laughed. "Dream on, pal. She's mine."

Wolf's eyes widened. "You want to bet?"

"Why not? Although I hate having to beat you."

"You won't. I'll fuck her first," Wolf said.

"I wouldn't be so sure of that, if I were you."

"Well what do you know? We're competing for a woman," Wolf said. "We've never done that before."

"First time for everything."

About the Author

ALICE GAINES loves her romance as hot as she can get it. Besides spinning tales in her head, Alice's passions include vegetable gardening, the San Francisco 49ers, and America's Test Kitchen. She's a maniacal fan of East Bay soul band Tower of Power.

Alice has a Ph.D. in psychology from the University of California at Berkeley and lives in Oakland, California, with her pet corn snake, Casper, and a strange cat that moved into her yard.